THE CULT OF THE LEOPARD!

"He senses blood, Mr. Carter. I believe it is your blood he smells. That is truly unfortunate. I shall have to kill him. No cat can remain in captivity who has tasted human blood."

"You're breaking my heart," I hissed.

A sadistic smile broke out on his lips. Carefully, with one eye still down the steps, he moved from the head of the stairway.

"Vadu has always been my favorite pet," he spat. "But since he must die, it is only fair he get a last meal. Please, Mr. Carter, I wish you to walk down those steps."

In answer, another rumbling roar carried up from the stairwell. My belly iced over at the thought of facing death at the leopard's jaws. . . .

NICK CARTER IS IT!

FROM THE NICK CARTER
          KILLMASTER SERIES

AND NEXT THE KING
CHECKMATE IN RIO
THE DAY OF THE DINGO
DEATH MISSION: HAVANA
DOOMSDAY SPORE
EIGHTH CARD STUD
THE GALLAGHER PLOT
THE JUDAS SPY
THE MAN WHO SOLD DEATH
THE NICHOVEV PLOT
PAMPLONA
THE PEMEX CHART
THE REDOLMO AFFAIR
THE SATAN TRAP
THE SIGN OF THE PRAYER SHAWL
STRIKE OF THE HAWK
SUICIDE SEAT
TARANTULA STRIKE
TEMPLE OF FEAR
TEN TIMES DYNAMITE
THUNDERSTRIKE IN SYRIA
TIME CLOCK OF DEATH
TRIPLE CROSS
TURKISH BLOODBATH
UNDER THE WALL
WAR FROM THE CLOUDS
THE WEAPON OF NIGHT

*Dedicated to the men of the
Secret Services of the
United States of America*

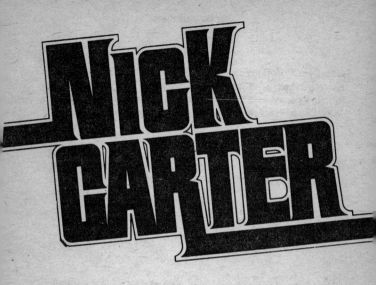

THE SOCIETY OF NINE

CHARTER
NEW YORK

A DIVISION OF CHARTER COMMUNICATIONS INC.
A GROSSET & DUNLAP COMPANY

SOCIETY OF NINE

A Charter Original.

First Charter Printing April 1981

Published simultaneously in Canada
Manufactured in the United States of America

2 4 6 8 0 9 5 3 1

CHAPTER ONE

Teeming wasn't the word for Algiers. Boiling was more apropos. Set between moderate Morocco to the east and Libya to the west, and slightly left of crazy, it boiled in the North African sun.

And I, Nick Carter, boiled along with it, even under the sidewalk canopy of the *Café Liberation*. Shielding my eyes were glasses of the darkest lens available, but I still squinted beneath them at the glaring sun as it danced off the multicolored tiles of the café's tiny veranda.

Hot?

Hell, yes, it was hot, making me all too aware of my own sweat as it seeped through the white linen of my shirt and painted dark patches across the slightly over-sized white jacket I was wearing.

I checked my issue wristwatch with the special doodads that did special things.

Three-twenty.

My contact was now twenty minutes late. That's never a pleasant omen, but then no reason to get the jitters, either. I downed the last few swallows of a sweet mint tea, and allowed my eyes to wander.

The surroundings were anything but frightening. The café itself covered most of the sidewalk of one of the large avenues leading into the Casbah. Around me sat a mixture of business types and tourists, none of whom showed any particular interest in me. All were either lost in their own conversations, or gaping at the endless parade of Arabs, Bedouins, and ass-pulled

1

carts plodding their wares up this final block to the walls of the old city.

In the distance I could hear that unmistakable potpourri of chatter and music that signified their goal. The Casbah, the world's oldest shopping center.

"Would the gentleman care for more tea?"

His voice took me three inches out of my chair.

As my eyes leaped up to his face, the waiter's puzzled expression quickly gave way to a smile that revealed random gaps where teeth should have been.

"More tea, *monsieur?*"

"Oh, yes! Yes, of course," I sighed, using French. The language had lasted, even though the French hadn't. "*Merci,* another tea, please."

He darted off, leaving me to gather up what remained of my composure.

Back to the watch.

Three twenty-two.

Clever, Carter. All of two minutes since you last checked. When you start looking once a minute, they hand you a gold-plated timepiece and retire you to a comfy condo in Florida.

Jumpy? Yeah, I was, and there were a lot of reasons for it. Not the least of which was Algiers itself.

My eyes rolled back to the dusty street and down to where it disappeared beneath a tiled arch in the old city wall.

I'd been to them all—Tangier, Rabat, Casablanca, Fez, even Qaddaffi's stronghold, Tripoli.

But Algiers was unique.

It was a haunting city, a casserole of mixed cultures that had been left baking in the sun for thousands of years, until it hardened into ceramic permanence. Anything that unchangeable has got to be just a little bit sinister.

But also mysterious . . . pleasantly mysterious.

Like the figures of two women walking up the avenue. Their long djellabas were barely rustling as they made their way through the moving humanity in short, petite strides. Their faces were covered, but the flashing onyx of their eyes beckoned like a muezzin calling the faithful to prayer.

I have always been a believer in the old adage that the female is most sensuous to the male when something is left to the imagination. On that basis, Muslim women win the championship, hands down. The men of Islam have immersed their women in a sea of garments, allowing only a tiny island of olive skin to peer out from behind their veils. And yet, in spite of their limited exposure, Arab women seem able to reach down within themselves and tell you volumes, using nothing more than their eyes.

Eyes so soft you could curl up in them.

As the two women neared my table, the one closest to me locked her eyes on mine. There was curiosity in her gaze, curiosity and incredible youth. I smiled and gave her a brief nod, fully expecting her to make an embarrassed retreat.

She didn't.

If anything, her look became even more penetrating. I stiffened slightly in my chair while the deep appraisal of her stare seemed to shoot right through me. A slight charge of adrenaline hit my spine, bringing with it the awareness that I just might be facing my contact.

I was just beginning a quick review of the agreed upon recognition procedures, when the spell was broken.

The second woman, suddenly realizing the intensity of contact between myself and her companion, straightened up and drove her elbow into the young

girl's shoulder. The youthful eyes left me, offered
meek apology to the older woman's glare, and returned
a humble perusal of the street before her.

I settled back once more, and once more consulted
the mocking face of my watch.

Three twenty-seven.

A five minute lapse. Better, Carter, much better.

I couldn't help a small chuckle of embarrassment.
How could I have mistaken eyes that innocent for my
contact? In all my years in this business, I had encountered hundreds of unknown faces, all with their own
veils of secrecy; but always the same eyes.

Hard eyes, never soft, like that girl's were. The eyes
I looked for were like chipped marble, that had no
warmth.

They were the same eyes I shaved with every morning.

There had been mystery in the young girl's eyes, but
no disguise. The people I dealt with all hid behind a
disguise; either of their own making or someone else's.

As I did now, in my own sweat, courtesy of Mr.
Willie Geis, New York.

Willie had two major characteristics: one, a wrist
you couldn't keep stiff with an iron bar, and two, a
genius for disguise that had saved my ass on more
occasions than I could recall.

With typical finesse, Willie had turned my hair
from its usual black, to the rusty red hue it now displayed. To this, he had added a moustache to match.
Then came the scar, starting at the end of my right
eyebrow and extending down across the cheekbone; a
scar so real a surgeon couldn't dispute it.

The final veil was provided by AXE. My identity:
Liam McDaniel, British citizen and Irish revolution-
ary.

"Your tea, *monsieur*."

"*Merci*." I pushed two dinars his way from the pile on the table in front of me.

"I make this tea special, *monsieur*, just for you, special."

I studied the waiter's dark-skinned face uncertainly. He was beaming like a schoolboy, his head alternating between bobbing encouragement and quick darts toward my cup.

With resignation I sipped at the steaming mixture he had brought. The pungent mint of the tea seemed to fill my head, but along with it came an unfamiliar bite. My palate struggled to identify the flavor, but with no success. Only one fact was clear.

Whatever he had thrown into the brew, it was alcoholic, and it was strong.

"To what do I owe this honor?" I gasped.

His smile got impossibly broader. "Algiers is to relax, *monsieur*. It is a city of life. I see you are not relaxed, *monsieur*, so I say . . . I relax him!" His smile drooped somewhat. "I did right, *monsieur*?"

"Yes," I chuckled. "You did very right!"

I added two more dinars to his side of the table and watched him bow away. I sat back, gratefully sipping the result of my waiter's generosity . . . and courage. This near the old town was very Muslim, and therefore very nonalcoholic. His ass could be slinged if the management caught him moving booze to natives or tourists.

Nothing had changed. The heat waves still danced their crazy patterns up from the street. I didn't let them hypnotize me, and concentrated beyond them, searching, looking for the unknown.

It was an occupational hazard, part of the business. The business?

I work for AXE, a supersecret branch of United States Intelligence. AXE is an elite club, whose select members carry the rating of "Killmaster". It's a club you don't get into easily, and you usually depart in a coffin, if they find enough pieces to fill one up. You don't spend as many years as I have maintaining your membership, and not learn to rely very heavily on your instincts.

My instincts were very clear: something about this mission smelled.

I took another sip of my spiked tea, and allowed my mind to recap all the events that had led me to the *Café Liberation*.

It was hard to believe this whole mess had started only three days earlier. I had just come off assignment in California. It seems some rather large quantities of fissionable material were making their way out of the nuclear power unit in San Onofre, and reappearing in Libyan vessels off the coast. As far as most missions go, this one was cleaned up rather easily; but I was still due for a week or two of R and R.

And that meant Pam MacMahon.

Pam had been a growing fascination of mine, one of those rare marriages of beauty and brains that could make a man start to think serious thoughts. Facially she was a study in chiseled excellence: perfectly sculpted bones, surrounded by a halo of dark, silky hair. Physically she was of medium height, with elegantly tapered limbs that bordered on slight. But however economical mother nature had been with Pam's torso, she had more than made up for it with a pair of huge breasts that danced teasingly beneath any garment that tried to cover them.

And they had been dancing so beautifully that afternoon three days before.

We were midway through an afternoon of tennis.

What with the antics beneath her blouse, and my expectations of the evening to come, she had me down two sets to one and was leading five games to love in the fourth.

I could not have cared less.

Twice before I had attempted to explore the promises in the lovely lady's eyes, and twice before the attempt had disintegrated in an emergency summons from Hawk. But not this time, I was determined.

She sent the ball sailing toward my backhand, and I took a bead on it. But a surprising twist of English turned it back into me; the best I could do was return it limply into the net.

Set and match.

I moved to the net to congratulate her, basking in the total radiance of her smile. She had teeth so perfect you could taste them.

I was about to, when I heard a car screech to a halt just beyond the courts.

I knew. Don't ask me how, I just knew. Without lifting my lips from the promise of hers, I rolled to peripheral vision and knew for sure.

Sedan. Dark blue with a radio that didn't play blues or rock. It played two-way, from the car to a line that hooked up to The Amalgamated Press And Wire Service.

Just like the logo on its side said.

But to me it said AXE, and I knew, want to or not, I was off again.

I muttered a brief apology to Pam, and went to meet the approaching driver. I anticipated the worst, and got it. Emergency summons: Code Red . . . Immediate.

That meant not even changing clothes, but I begged a few seconds reprieve to present my excuses to the lady. No sooner had I turned around, however, than I saw her racquet bouncing off the court and her sweet buttocks charging out through the opposite gate in the chain link fence.

I sighed, the driver shrugged, and together we made the silent journey to Dupont Circle, the home of AXE and its dedicated creator, David Hawk.

Dejectedly, I entered the outer office and found Hawk's secretary, Ginger Bateman, standing over her filing cabinet.

Ginger was as firm and as fleshy as the peaches her home state was famous for producing. But she also wore an armor over that flesh that was harder and far colder than steel. I'd dented it once, and even put a couple of chinks in it, but I'd never penetrated it.

If anything or anyone could be better endowed than the lady I had just left, it was Ginger. That was why it was so painful when she took one look at me and started rippling with laughter. Those ripples did things to her chest that made me remember what I was missing at that very moment with Pam MacMahon.

"You're laughing," I said.

"I can't help it."

"Why?"

"Something just hit me."

"Like?"

"You look like you just came in from a rerun of 'I Spy!' "

I gave a quick glance to the tennis outfit I still wore, and searched vainly for a comeback.

"Smart ass," was unfortunately the best I could produce.

She must have sensed my mood, because her next move was to walk over, put her arms around me, and give me a light peck on the lips.

"Oh, honey," she purred, throwing every ounce of her Southern upbringing into her voice. "Why, ah declare, Ashley Masters, you do seem to be in quite a state. Now don't y'all worry none. Mah dance card is yours at the next cotillion, ya heah?''

In spite of myself, a small smile creased my lips. I stared down into the dark valley of cleavage between her breasts, and felt Pam's image fog slightly in my mind.

"Why, thank y'all, Louella-Lee." I did my best to match her syrupy southern elegance. "Does this mean ah can be your beau?"

She laughed appreciatively, pressing herself even tighter against me. "Well, ah don't rightly know, Ashley . . . but it does mean you can enter my gazebo anytime y'all want.''

The glint in her eye left no doubt as to her meaning, and Pam took three more giant steps toward being a memory. Once more I wondered why it was that I had never tried to get to know Ginger outside of AXE's somber surroundings.

As our mutual enjoyment ebbed, I thought I could sense the same question lingering in her mind. It became even more pronounced as the laughter of our joking echoed off, leaving only the soft reality of our touching bodies.

Pam who?

I moved my hands around until I could cup her soft buttocks. "What are you doing for the next hour?"

"Having lunch," she intoned, "with the secretary of the Secretary of State . . . right after I let you into the boss's office.''

"Did you ever do it in the back seat of a Chevy when you were a little girl?"

"No, darling . . . when I was a big girl. And it was a Cadillac.''

A buzzer sounded and Hawk's voice barked over the intercom. "Bateman, get him in here!"

"How does he know?" I asked.

"I dunno," she replied, "but he always does . . . doesn't he?"

"Always."

I reluctantly broke away, composing my thoughts for their entry into Hawk's inner sanctum. As I neared the door, Ginger's voice halted me.

"Nick?"

"Yeah." I turned.

An impish smile broke across her lovely face as she gestured toward my tennis shorts. "Nice buns!" Her eyebrows began leaping up and down like a poor man's Groucho Marx.

"Bitch." I moved through the door into Hawk's office, doing my best to erase the smirk on my face.

I entered and was immediately hit with three different sensations. One, the familiar smells of leather, mahogany, and cigar smoke that always permeated David Hawk's office; two, the chiseled features and flinty eyes of David Hawk himself; and three, the unexpected presence of a third party.

My gloom quickly turned into relief and pleasure as the stranger's features registered. It was Davidson Harcourt, one of the finest minds British Intelligence ever nurtured. We had crossed paths many times in joint U.S.-British ventures, but mostly at opposite ends of his desk. Only once had I worked with him in the field, and his tradecraft proved to be as agile and creative as his mind.

Harcourt's frail body, diminished even more by the muted suit he wore, rose to greet me. His eyes revealed their own delight, magnified behind the thick-lensed spectacles he always wore. He thrust his slender hand out toward me.

"I say, old man, good to see you!" he said. "Doing well, I see. Yes, very well indeed."

"Definitely," I replied. "Very well indeed."

I clasped his proffered hand with the care one would give an injured bird. It was one of those things about Harcourt; that you always acknowledged his frailty when, in reality, he could take all you had to give.

That was how he survived . . . in a business of survival.

"Obviously no need for introductions." It was Hawk's rasping voice. He too had risen, more in deference to his guest than me, I was sure, but the tone in his voice let us all know that it was a time for business and not reunions.

The three of us settled into chairs, and I awaited the stern tones of Hawk's briefing.

It didn't take long.

"Sorry to pull you off leave, N-3. It's irregular, I know, but this one just sort of dropped in on us. I'm sure you'll see the necessity as we move along."

"I understand, sir. It must be important."

"It is," Hawk assured. "I suppose it would be best if Harcourt filled you in on his end first."

"Yes, of course," said the Englishman as he shifted in his chair and opened the briefcase lying on the floor next to him.

"It all came about two days ago," he began. "It seems there was a little case of hit and run in one of the shabbier sections of Soho. Chap's name was Liam McDaniel."

Harcourt paused to retrieve a dossier, and handed it over to me before continuing.

"The local constables traced down his flat, and did a routine search, of course. But it seems he possessed a number of rather unroutine items. You'll see them listed about midpage."

My eyes shot down to the bracketed listing. It was unroutine indeed. (ONE BRITISH MADE SNIPER'S RIFLE, CUSTOM-BORED, WITH FULL BREAK-

DOWN CAPACITY; ONE SNIPER'S SCOPE WITH
INFRA-RED ADAPTER; ONE RIFLE SILENCER;
SIX EXPLODING SHELLS)

I whistled softly. "Reads like the main booth at an
assassin's flea market," I muttered.

"Precisely, Nicholas," replied the Englishman.
"Fortunately, the constables felt the same way. What
with the magnitude of this chap's little arsenal, and the
fact that his room was papered with news clippings of
various terrorist attacks and threats, the local chaps felt
inclined to contact our antiterror branch."

Harcourt paused briefly to pull out his pipe and
tobacco pouch. I used the brief pause to re-review the
list before me.

You can tell a lot about a killer by his choice of
hardware. The weapon itself says volumes. A simple
hand gun or plain rifle say one of two things about their
user: one, he's an amateur, or two, he's expendable.
The scope implies at least a certain concern for survival; it creates distance. The silencer implies more;
distance *and* secrecy, and at least enough confusion as
to source and location to offer some hope of escape.

The fine print woven throughout the listing offered
even greater insight. The rifle: special bore, with custom tailoring on the sights. Definitely professional.
The rifle had breakdown capacity: a sign of individual
tastes. The man felt comfortable with his own weapon,
and was willing to risk transport to use it. *Very* professional.

The bullets made their own statement. While
weapons talk about their users, shells reveal targets.
There are two ways in which the human animal can
suffer from the impact of a bullet. Vital organs can be
hit, and thereby bring on death, or the projectile can
miss the desired organs, but create such internal shock
that the target will perish. Messy, but effective.

Exploding shells had already terminated several of my friendships, and at least two other N-rated killmasters that I had known. They have the unique capacity of virtually exploding upon contact, thereby taking forty-to-sixty percent more of the human body with them than conventional shells would. I had personally watched six people die from what should have amounted to no more than a shoulder or leg wound.

Whoever the man's target was, his death was obviously very important.

My gaze returned to Harcourt, his pipe churning out the custom blended aroma of Turkish and vanilla tobaccos by which I had come to recognize his presence. His voice, creeping around the pipe stem, was not without irony.

"I believe the phrase is, 'heavy duty,' what?"

I could only nod in agreement.

"There's something else, Nicholas. The antiterrorist boys moved in, and gave the flat a rather more thorough look-see. They managed to dig up this."

Harcourt reached once more into his briefcase and held up a rather worn, frayed notebook.

"It seems the gent kept a diary, in rather clumsy code. Easy enough for the crypto chaps to break down. Let me give you a transcript."

The notebook found its way back into the briefcase, and he handed over to me a large sheaf of typed pages. I scanned them briefly.

"I think you'll find the bloke was really quite candid about himself, but more to the point, he seems to have been biding his time awaiting contact and instructions."

"An I.R.A. hit?" I asked.

"We thought so at first, so we placed someone in the flat and waited to see what would creep out of the woodwork. The results were rather surprising."

Harcourt pulled out another bundle from the case. "These arrived the next day, by regular post." He handed the pile over to me.

It consisted of several shipping documents, all in seeming order, and a typed sheet of instructions for the export of a small consignment of religious goods to be sent to Capetown, South Africa.

"The hardware?" I inquired.

"Has to be," he nodded. "The shipper has been checked. He's not too fussy about the goods he handles, but nothing big time."

The rest of the bundle amounted to no more than a plane ticket to Algiers, and another typed sheet of contact procedures.

"Once the antiterrorist chaps were certain that there were no immediate domestic concerns, they turned it over to us. The South African company to which the guns are being shipped is, of course, a bogus. Probably McDaniel himself would take possession of the consignment." Harcourt leaned forward in the chair and took a thoughtful puff on the pipe. "We then tried to get some information on McDaniel himself. Rather an enigma, that one. He is, of course, Anglo-Irish by birth, and not without strong affinities for the I.R.A. cause. But his real emotions seem to cleave to *any* of what he considers to be the world's oppressed peoples."

"A freelancer?" I offered.

"I would appear so, yes," Harcourt nodded, another explosion of smoke curling out from his pipe. "But that's the first thing that grew to bother me."

"What's that?"

"Well," he paused, his eyes narrowing, "as you well know, Nicholas, most assassins are really quite identifiable . . . by style and execution, if not always by face. It's their way of signing their work. But

McDaniels has proved something of a puzzle. His equipment is quite individual, as you can see . . . special bored rifle, trimmed sights, etc. Really quite an assemblage for someone we can produce no record on.''

I found myself sharing his confusion. ''No make on him at all?''

''Not a jot. Nothing with Interpol or any of our sister intelligence agencies. Seems the lad is little more than driftwood that suddenly washed up on our shores. And that's the second thing that bothers me. With so many pros on the market, why go with a rookie?''

''Anything on his employer?'' I asked.

''Nothing specific,'' he answered, shaking his head. ''Our only real link was through the chap doing the shipping. We rousted him a bit, but all he could tell us was that the arrangements were made through some black fellow . . . heavily accented, and by the sound of it, as South African as the shipping address.''

I had to agree with Harcourt, it was too many loose ends in a business that usually wraps itself in the tightest of knots.

''But why come to us?'' I asked. ''It looks like a colonial affair to me.''

''Two reasons, actually. First of all, the colonials get a bit testy when we poke our noses into their little show. They like to think it's none of our bloody business. We ignore it, of course, but we do try to be discreet. However, in our attempts to run this little mystery down, we did stumble onto certain hints that perhaps you Yanks had something brewing down there. Something big, by the look of it.''

Harcourt's eyes drifted over to Hawk's face. If he hoped to catch a glimmer of reaction, he was disappointed. Hawk's features were like an iron mask.

''At any rate,'' he continued, ''it began to look as if

it might concern your company more than ours, and we thought we'd let you know about it.''

"Appreciate it, Harcourt.'' It was the first sound from Hawk since the briefing began.

''Nothing, really. We chaps have to look out for each other, wouldn't you say?''

Hawk merely nodded.

"And the second reason?'' I asked.

Harcourt reached once more into his bottomless briefcase. ''It rather speaks for itself,'' he said, chuckling slightly and handing over a photo to me. "Wouldn't you say, old boy?''

I looked down at the photograph. The man in it was lying in the street, the rather surprised look of death on his face. And then I saw it. The look on my own face could not have been any less surprised.

"McDaniel?'' I gasped.

"Indeed, my good fellow,'' came Harcourt's reply. "Uncanny, what?''

I had no reply. With the exception of the red hair, red moustache, and the scar down his face, I was looking at a perfect double of none other than yours truly.

A carbon copy of Nick Carter!

CHAPTER TWO

I could only stare in stunned silence. If Mama Carter had a baby boy that no one knew of, I was staring at him. It was eerie, made even more eerie by the fact that he was lying dead in a Soho street.

I was hardly aware of Harcourt's departure from the room. The best I could muster were a few grunting acknowledgments of his polite retreat. It was Hawk's own voice, now returned to his position behind the desk, that finally brought me back to reality.

"Spooky, isn't it?" His teeth were clamped over a freshly lit cigar.

"At least," was all I could reply. I paused only long enough to catch my breath. "What's the story?"

Hawk smiled slightly. "I have good news, and bad news."

I nodded. "Let's try the good news first." I dropped the pile of goodies Harcourt had laid on me, picture and all, onto Hawk's desk and sat back for the briefing.

"Well," he growled. "In the first place, there is indeed a deal going on in South Africa; a real sweet deal, if we can pull it off. As I'm sure you're aware, the black representation issue is South Africa's biggest hernia."

Again I nodded.

Hawk leaned back into his huge chair. "And, as I'm sure you're also aware, the black issue has been Russia's invitation for activities in Africa's southern horn."

Another nod.

"What I'm sure you don't know, is that recently we've made some substantial progress; covert, of course, but very substantial indeed. As Harcourt so subtlely implied, things are cooking for us."

"Big?" I asked.

Hawk smiled again. "Christmas dinner," he beamed.

His joy was infectious. I felt myself smiling even through the huge question marks in my brain. "Do I get an invitation?"

Hawk leaned forward, patted the pile of papers I had placed on his desk. "Looks like you might be the guest of honor."

"Then I better know the guest list."

"Excellent." He rose and began pacing the office. "Are you familiar with Joseph Nikumba?"

I searched the file cabinet in my memory bank. "Kind of," I replied. "One of the head honchos in the black movement, isn't he?" Low key, but his name does creep out in the papers now and again."

"He's a lot more than that," Hawk said. "At the moment, at least from our point of view, he's probably the only key we've got for opening the door to South Africa."

"He sure keeps a low profile," I offered.

Hawk allowed himself a chuckle. "We like it that way. Actually, keeping him out of the papers has been relatively easy. He doesn't wave a gun, he's never killed any Anglos, and he would look ridiculous in battle fatigues. He's a simple professor. As a result, the South African press won't touch him because he won't scare the whites, and the international wire services are convinced he'd bore their readers to tears. He's just not the stuff that boosted circulation rates are made of."

"Pity," I chimed.

"Yeah," added Hawk, plopping himself onto the

end of his desk. He withdrew the cigar from his mouth, and picked lightly at the stray strands of tobacco that were creeping out from its shredded end. He was almost nonchalant as he continued.

"What he *is*, however, is the biggest hope we've ever had of seeing black rule in South Africa . . .*effective* black rule, with the Russians packing for home." A wad of tobacco strands found their way emphatically into the wastebasket.

"I like him already," I said, pulling out one of my own custom cigarettes. "And exactly how is he going to pull it off?"

"Glad you asked that," Hawk said, as he resumed his pacing. "As you may be aware, the problem with most black takeovers in African government—peaceful or not, communist or not—is the blacks themselves. Or, more specifically, the black tribal structures in African culture."

Hawk's energy level was switching into second gear, as I lit my cigarette.

"When the colonial powers moved into Africa, they divided up the pie to suit their own interests. Borders and countries were agreed upon, with no concern being given to the tribal divisions that have existed since time began. As a result, Africa has become a boiling pot of tribal rivalries and jealousies. The colonial powers gave these arbitrary divisions names, and called them countries. And now, no matter which one gains its independence, its history seems to become one big contest as to which tribe will control the reins; usually to the detriment of every other tribe, and usually to the meddlesome delight of the Soviet Union."

I nodded my understanding. So far I was getting African History: 101. "And how does Nikumba figure in?"

Hawk paused in his pacing and smiled; the kind of

smile I had seen on rare occasions, usually when I had pulled some mission from the jaws of defeat into victory, even if it was by the seat of my pants.

"Remarkable individual," he mused, chewing on his cigar. "Here's his bio." Hawk reached onto his desk to hand me the folder. I scanned it while he filled me in.

"Briefly, it runs like this. As I said, he's a professor, with two degrees: one, a doctorate in social anthropology from the University of Johannesburg, and two, a doctorate in psychology from Oxford."

I was impressed with the credentials.

Hawks continued. "He has been blessed with a unique upbringing. His father had gotten an unusually good missionary education, and found himself in a small government post in one of those occasional token gestures the South African government makes to keep the blacks from bitching too loudly. This enabled Nikumba to get a better than average shot at his own schooling."

"And he apparently used it," I added.

"Indeed," nodded Hawk. "But he never forgot where he came from. His sympathies always seemed to embrace the black cause, in spite of the fact that he had managed to escape the worst of it. Early on in his education, he came to a relatively startling conclusion. If tribal differences were what was tearing Africa apart, then tribal *similarities* just might be what would pull it back together."

"Let me guess," I offered. "So he studied social anthropology, made a broad survey of South African tribal cultures, and has since come up with a formula of how to blend them all together in peace and harmony."

"Bright boy," Hawk smiled. "That is exactly what he has done."

I took a drag on my cigarette, allowing the information to filter through my brain. "Nice theory," I said finally. "But can it really be pulled off in practice? I mean, that's a lot of cultural material to try to toss into one stew."

Hawk paused in his ramblings to perch once more on his desk. "Not all that many, really. That's the interesting thing. "There are a lot of local tribal variations, yes. But they all derive from the same cultural stock. The majority of black Africans in South Africa—and I'm referring not just to the country, but the whole of sub-Saharan Africa itself—are all merely branches of the same basic tree; they're *all* Bantu."

The picture was beginning to clear up. "What you're saying is, he studied each of these Bantu peoples, threw out the differences, and held onto the root similarities that they all have in common?"

Hawk nodded as I continued.

"The thing I still don't get is that, if all these tribes are basically off the same assembly line, why are they slitting each others' throats?"

Hawk's tone became almost chiding, like a schoolmaster rebuking a recalcitrant student. "Don't minimize those differences, Nick. They may seem to be minor . . . no more severe, say, than the difference between a Georgian's mint julep and a New Englander's clam chowder. But there was a time, not too God-awful long ago, when that same Georgian would have blown that New Englander's head off with small provocation."

I got the point.

"Can he pull it off?" I asked.

"He already is. He's done some incredible field work with some of the more remote tribes, and natives that were once drying each other's heads for centerpieces are now swapping tom-toms and bowling on the same leagues."

"Well, that's great for the blacks," I added. "But he still has to get the colonials to hand over the government. The cultural differences here are a little more vast. The last I heard, a black could get his head blown off for merely smiling."

"True," Hawk said. "And that's where we come in." He moved around and returned himself to the chair behind his desk. "Do you know anything about Namibia?" he asked, taking his seat.

I dove once more into the memory bank. Namibia is the new African name for the country previously known as South-West Africa. Theoretically, it's an independent nation, at least as far as the United Nations is concerned. In 1968, the U.N. issued a charter granting South-West Africa (or Namibia) full independence, but the reality is that it is totally controlled by the South African government.

And for good reason.

Namibia is one of the world's richest gold and diamond producers.

With that much wealth lying around in the ground, it was little wonder that the South African government had risked all manner of sanctions to retain control. Better to have that kind of wealth flowing into ones own coffers, than to allow it its own freedom of spending.

I shared my knowledge with Hawk, and he embellished on it.

"That is indeed the situation. About a year ago, Nikumba wandered into one of our South African CIA branches and asked to speak to the station chief. We were a bit startled, to say the least, but surprise gave way to salivation as he laid out one of the sweetest deals we had heard to date."

The smoke was pouring from his mouth like a train as Hawk moved his energy into third gear.

"He was very direct in what he wanted. Black rule in

South Africa is merely a matter of time. The only real question is what kind of government it's going to be, and who's going to be running the show. Left to his own devices, Nikumba knows that he'd probably never see more than an advisory position in any newly engendered regime. There just don't seem to be too many social anthropologists running countries these days. The control goes to the guys in the bushes, with the guns and fatigues.''

"And Nikumba feels he could do better, right?"

"He can!" Hawk's voice took on that chiding tone again. "In the first place, he's the only man on Earth who could win the support of *all* blacks, and bridge their tribal differences enough to forge a real nation, *without* violent measures. But on top of that, he is more than interested in retaining the niceties of life that the colonials have brought into his African world."

I ventured a guess. "And that means hanging onto Namibia?"

"Exactly," Hawk nodded, his cigar thrusting toward me in emphasis. "There is a pattern to the birthing of African nations, and Nikumba is desperate to avoid it. Basically it runs like this: A country gets born, with one of its noble freedom fighters at the helm. The blacks are jubilant and optimistic, while the whites get scared and pack up for greener pastures. With them usually goes the economic future of the country. Progress grinds to a halt, the once jubilant population becomes restless, the once noble freedom fighter starts getting testy, and the Russians ooze in to keep everybody at each other's throats. Suddenly, bang. Before you can say Patrice Lumumba, there's a revolution, and the Commies own themselves another hunk of Africa. Nobody's any happier, of course, but now, if you complain, your mother turns you in to the KGB."

Hawk's eyes suddenly seemed to catch fire.

"Nikumba offered us a way around this. His deal was simple. America was to throw its complete support behind a Nikumba-run black African government. Our commitment was to be total . . . economically, industrially, technologically, and, if need be, militarily. It was originally hoped that such a strong show of support from us would help to alleviate some of the white colonials' fears in regard to a black takeover."

"Has it?" I asked.

Hawk grinned once more. "The man isn't a doctor of psychology for nothing. There was a brief period of resentment over America poking its nose into other people's business, et cetera, et cetera. But that quickly gave way to a delightfully heartwarming explosion of white optimism. Once the colonials realized that life would be "business-as-usual", at least as far as their pocketbooks were concerned, they warmed up to both Nikumba and us with an enthusiasm I can only call ferocious."

Hawk's earlier phrase flashed through my mind. "Christmas dinner," I mumbled.

"What?"

"Nothing. Go on."

Hawk popped up, and resumed a pacing flight pattern around the office. "It is Nikumba's belief that by mollifying white fears, and hanging onto the Namibian assets, he can avoid the usual cycle of economic rise and fall that seems to accompany every African regime."

"And what's the game plan?" I asked.

"At the moment," he answered, "it's to keep things as quiet as possible. We've got the support of all the people, black or white, who really have a say in things. It's just a question of how to feed it to the masses."

I took a final drag on my cigarette and retired it, as Hawk continued.

"The basic plan is simple enough: heavy monetary and industrial involvement in Namibia and South Africa. Several corporations are even now beginning their moves into these areas . . . with some incredibly lucrative gold and diamond deals for incentive. It is hoped that this involvement will reassure the white population that there will be no black backlash. More importantly, it is hoped that this will also tie South Africa and Namibia together in a chain of mutual economics that will become difficult to sever."

So far it all sounded feasible.

"From that point," he continued, "it is just a matter of time until Nikumba is given power. At that moment, we begin the campaign to have him recognized unilaterally."

In spite of the seriousness of Hawk's manner, I was forced to chuckle. "That doesn't sound too difficult. You show me a United Nations representative that won't support a black-ruled African government, and I'll show you a candidate for instant retirement."

"There's no problem in getting recognition, per se. What's going to take real orchestration is to get the rest of the world to recognize South Africa's sovereignty over Namibia.

"The immediate benefits are obvious. World recognition of the new black government will release South Africa from the various trade embargoes and restrictions their previous aparthied policy has brought on, opening them, and Nikumba, to a world economy. If successful, the retention of Namibia will give them an almost virtual monopoly on gold and diamonds—a powerful base, indeed, from which to greet their new world market."

"Then, at this point," I said, picking up the thread, "Nikumba will divert the greater portion of this new-found wealth into Namibia itself, thereby creating a surge of public projects and benefits that will both tighten the economic bond between them, and give meteoric rise to the Namibian standard of living.''

"That's the scenario. It is hoped," Hawk continued, "that the economic boon, plus his own charismatic power over the blacks in all of southern Africa, will win South Africa a mandate of power from the Namibian peoples themselves . . . in open election.''

It was a sweet deal, indeed. Africa was rapidly becoming the world's biggest battleground between us and the Communist world. To have a foothold in a country that expansive, and that mineral-rich, was a coup not to be taken lightly.

I returned my attention to Hawk, but nothing was forthcoming. He had wandered over to the window at the far end of the room, and seemed to be staring out in deep thought. His cigar was poking out from his face, and I watched about three inches of neglected ash drop off and splatter onto his shoe, before I allowed myself to break the spell.

"I take it that's the good news.''

He turned, his cigar readied for more abuse. "Yep. That's the good news.''

"Let's hear the bad.''

Hawk's features darkened somewhat. "I think we've got a leak on the negotiating team.''

The words had a mournful echo to them. In the intelligence game, nothing can deaden you more than the knowledge that the other guy has a photocopy of your game plan.

"How certain are we?" I asked.

"About ninety percent.''

I winced. "Yeah," I sighed, "that's pretty certain.''

Hawk moved slowly from the window and resumed his seat at the desk. "We're really sticking our necks out on this one, Nick. Any leak could hurt us, and if it's as high up as it's beginning to look, it could be deadly. It would be one thing if just South Africa were involved. We win, they lose, and Moscow chalks it off as the breaks of the game.''

"I take it Namibia is the rub," I said.

"Rub!" Hawk let out with a disgusted sigh. "Sandblasting is more like it. The group fighting for Namibian independence is called the South-West African Peoples Organization, affectionately referred to as S.W.A.P.O. And they're up to their afros in Russian support. But what makes this so tricky is, this time we're not playing by the rules.''

"How so?"

"Normally, we pick our group, they pick theirs, and we both sit back to see who wins. But Nikumba wants us in . . . *directly* involved, and if Moscow gets mad enough, they just might do the same thing.''

The full implications were beginning to hit me. "And because of the United Nations charter, any reactionary move the Russians made would have to be at least tacitly supported by the world community.''

Hawk nodded his agreement. "Like it or not, world opinion is behind them, for once. It's a time bomb, Nick. If we bring in the marines, they can too, and if we start bumping heads down there, I won't give it a month till it starts moving out across the globe.''

There was a momentary flash where my belly turned to ice.

"Our only hope is to keep one step ahead of them, tiptoe our way through some rather shaky negotiations, and wait for Nikumba to win the Namibian mandate.''

"And we can't do that," I added, "if Ivan's sitting right in the middle of our huddle.''

"You got it.''

"Any clues as to where the leak is coming from?"

Hawk shook his head. "Not yet. It's been too

gradual a progression to get a fix on. At first, the Russians merely stepped up activities in the area. With something this big, it's nearly impossible to keep an iron lid on things, and we just assumed they were working on rumors. But then, very slowly, they began popping up more frequently. It began to seem like every time we turned a corner, Ivan was waiting for us. We could no longer ignore the fact that information was seeping out from relatively high up the ladder.''

Hawk stubbed out the remains of his cigar and took a deep breath, exhaling slowly.

''And then came the real bad news. Two days ago we received information that no less than Yuri Berenko himself has moved into Africa.''

Yuri Berenko was one of the KGB's most shining lights. There were even rumors, solid ones indeed, that he was next in line to inherit the whole KGB operation. For Berenko to be called from his desk and put into the field was the espionage equivalent of the mountain going to Mohammed.

''It is my considered opinion,'' Hawk went on, ''that you only bring out the big guns when you know you've got a war on your hands.''

''And if he's running someone on our team,'' I added, ''they're high up the ladder, without a doubt.''

''And now this!'' Hawk snapped, his hand slamming onto Harcourt's files. ''We're vulnerable, Nick. All our strategy is pinned on one man: Nikumba. He's the only one who can pull the blacks together, and he's the only one the whites will swing for. Remove him from the picture, and the whole operation falls apart.''

I began to catch his drift. ''You think Nikumba may have McDaniel's target?''

''I don't know,'' he sighed. ''But we can't afford to overlook anything going into South Africa at the moment.''

"Could the Russians have hired McDaniel?"

Hawk ran a tensed hand across his brow before answering. "Not likely. They usually handle their own affairs. They don't need to go shopping for help. But it's always a possibility. McDaniels was a British citizen, and should he kill Nikumba, there would be little difficulty in making it look far more racist than political. Moscow could erase both Nikumba and the operation in one stroke, and there isn't a damn word we could say about it."

An ominous silence descended while both of us thought. It was as if we were trying to reverse events by force of will alone. Finally I said:

"What do you want me to do, boss?"

The reality of action seemed to pick up Hawk's spirits. "Obviously, you are to assume McDaniel's identity."

He reached into his top desk drawer and withdrew two airline tickets. He tossed the first down on my side of the desk.

"First, you are to go to New York and visit Willie Geis. I'm sure that by the time he's finished with you you'll look more like McDaniel than McDaniel did. As far as the man himself, the diary should provide you with all the background you may need. His employers are as ignorant of him as you are, so there shouldn't be any hang-ups on that score."

The second ticket jumped from Hawk's hand to cover the first. "From New York you'll head to London, and from there you'll pick up McDaniel's itinerary, just as it was given to him."

"Some contact must have already been made. Is there any danger of my being blown to the hiring agent?"

Hawk shook his head no. "Not likely. The diary indicates that the actual hiring was handled in one meeting. Both parties seemed equally concerned over their own anonymity. The contact was very brief, and all business. Put enough of the old English into your accent, and I doubt that anyone will spot the switch.''

"So be it.''

I stood up and collected the various items littering Hawk's desk. I paused to stare once more at the photo of McDaniel. The similarity was just too coincidental. The first nagging glimmer of doubt began working its way into my system. Hawk must have sensed it.

"Be careful, Nick,'' he murmured. "Track this down as far as it goes. If it looks like it'll hurt us, do whatever you have to to wrap it up. But if it doesn't affect us one way or the other, get the hell out as fast as you can.''

I nodded my agreement and headed for the door. Hawk's voice halted me.

"One more thing. I think we'll find our leak very quickly. But keep your ears open. If McDaniels was to become involved in this whole affair, you may hear some information that will help us to narrow down our suspects.''

"Both ears *and* both eyes will be wide open, I assure you,'' I replied grimly, shutting the door behind me and heading for the airport and Willie Geis, the nagging doubts growing in my brain.

CHAPTER THREE

By the time I reached Algiers, those nagging doubts had grown into a bundle of raw nerves that I found impossible to shake. Not even the biting comfort of the alcohol in my last swallow of tea could still the churnings in my gut.

I knew the waiter would be heartbroken.

I turned and scanned the cafe to see if he was nearby. The thought occurred that maybe one more of his special brews might just drown my nerves, but I then thought better of it. This was no time to be dulling whatever edge my senses retained.

I got my thoughts and my eyes back on the street, and was rewarded immediately.

When she first turned the corner, I shot up in my chair. She looked for all the world like Pam MacMahon. The hair was the same dark mantle, the features equally classic, and the body just as elegant.

But then the differences became apparent. I relaxed back into my chair and gave this approaching madonna the interest she deserved.

Her features were fuller than Pam's, very Caucasian, but the rich darkness of her skin hinted at a drop or two of black blood in her ancestry. Her breasts were smaller than Pam's, but still ample. They were incredibly firm, and showed themselves defiantly beneath the yellow of her silk blouse. Her legs, too, were fuller, with the kind of rounded, muscular definition that implied they could wrap themselves around you, and never let go.

I found myself reaching a conviction. Arab women

may be mysterious, and the imagination may be stimulating, but seeing is better.

She was very near my table when our eyes locked. As with the young Arab girl earlier, she held my gaze; there was no retreat. But unlike that earlier encounter, I experienced no surge of adrenaline. She was not my contact. It wasn't in her eyes.

Hers were ripe-olive color and expressive, not marbles.

I disengaged myself and turned to try to find my waiter. I located him at one of the far tables and was about to motion for his attention, when I felt a tap at my shoulder. I turned around, prepared for anything but what greeted me.

Above me, in all her glory, stood the madonna.

Her voice was as full and rich as her figure. "Sorry to trouble you, but I seem to need a match." As she spoke, she thrust up the box that held her cigarettes. It was an ordinary box of English Ovals, with one exception. There was a blank space, without printing, about one and a half inches square, on its face.

The madonna had just initiated step one in the recognition process. It took a second or two to pull myself together before I could offer my part.

"Yes, of course," I muttered. "No bother at all, luv."

I pulled a matchbook out from my coat pocket, and fired up one of the matches. I was careful to carry the matchbook up with me when I lit her cigarette. She studied it quickly. Glued to the front of the matchbook was the missing square from the face of her English Ovals box. Her eyes returned to my face and showed their acceptance.

"You're sure it's no bother?" she breathed.

I returned the matches to my pocket. "Only slight, luv. But if you'd allow me to buy you a drink, I'm certain it would be more than compensated.'' My accent was pure Yorkshire pudding.

She nodded, smiled, and made her way around to my table.

It was done. To anyone watching, it was a simple encounter; to us, it was the beginning of the game.

She seated herself across from me, and wasted no time in getting on with it. Her face held a winning smile, but her voice and attitude were all business.

"I take it there was no problem in the shipment of religious articles?'' Her accent was definitely colonial.

"None, luv. But then, I wasn't hired because I make mistakes, now was I?''

Her face registered slight irritation, but the smile held firm. "I really wouldn't know,'' she cooed. "Shall we get on with it?''

"Whatever you say, luv." I got the distinct feeling she didn't like me.

She reached into her purse and pulled out an envelope. She slipped it onto the table, her eyes darting nervously around the café.

"Take this,'' she said, inching it toward me. "Inside you'll find instructions, a hotel key and a plane ticket. Also some money.''

I leaned onto the table to collect her offering. As discreetly as possible, I slipped it into the inside pocket of my sports coat.

She continued. "You are to spend tonight in the hotel. In the morning you are to check out, and make the flight indicated on the ticket. I shall also be on the flight, but you are not to acknowledge me. Once at your destination, you will follow the instructions as indicated, to your hotel. I will be in the adjoining room. You will then be given further orders.''

"And just where is it I'm going, luvy?''

A momentary glare broke through her smiling

façade. Her voice was icy cold. "South Africa. Capetown, to be precise." Suddenly her eyes leaped up and her voice took on a tone of casual friendliness. "And I'll be staying in Algiers until tomorrow. How about yourself?"

The sudden appearance of the waiter explained the change.

"As a matter of fact, I'll be departing on the morrow also. Perhaps we could share our final evening together, what? Might I buy you a drink?"

"I'd love it. What do you recommend?"

I looked up into the waiter's face. His mouth was twisted in an idiotic grin, and his right eye kept fluttering in what I could only assume was a series of appreciative winks. He was undoubtedly convinced he had found the reason for my earlier case of nerves.

"I say, luv, why don't we let the waiter bring us two of his special teas."

He gave me a hasty thumbs up, and raced off to fill the order.

I leaned in closer over the table, and gave her my best leer. "Well now, that doesn't sound like such a bad idea at that. What say we turn the town a bit tonight? It'll give us a chance to get to know one another."

This time the glare totally defeated the smile. "I think not!" The ice was back in full force.

I studied her for a moment. The idea of spending the evening with her had obvious advantages, but my real interest was in getting some answers to the questions rolling around in my brain. She was the first question. Her attitude was all business, but underneath it all was fear. It showed in her constantly darting eyes, and in the shake of her hand as she puffed on her cigarette.

She just didn't read *pro*.

Again I went for her eyes. Soft. Much too soft. They

were timid, almost doe-like, and they were helpless to hide the cauldron of fear bubbling away inside her.

It was time to give it another try.

"Look, luv, just because we're doing a bit of business, it doesn't mean we can't work up a bit of fun too, does it?"

There was venom in her reply. "Look, Mr. McDaniel. The people I work for require your services, and as much as I detest it, I am to be an instrument in furthering that desire. But the desire is *theirs*, Mr. McDaniel, not mine, and I think it best that we have as little to do with each other as possible."

"Now, luvy . . ."

"And if you call me luvy one more time, I'm going to take my foot and relocate your balls."

It was my turn to switch on the ice. "Do that, *dearie*, and I will personally take that gorgeous leg of yours and tie it into knots."

A stare-down ensued, and the certainty of my threat was clearly established. Fear, once again, inhabited her eyes. The mood hovered slightly through the reappearance of our waiter and on into several sips of tea.

The silence seemed more devastating to her than the words.

"All right," I finally muttered. "If luvy ain't your favorite word, give me a name to play with."

She stared for a moment. "Robin," she said, a choke catching in her throat. "Robin Brenton."

"All right, Miss Brenton. If you don't feel like being chummy, that's your tea cake. I can do very nicely without friends, but I get just a bit nervous when I'm without answers. So far, your mates have kept me a trifle too much in the dark as to what I'm about, and I'd like for you to shed a little light on the picture."

Her eyes were darting again.

She was beginning to get to me. Once the game had started, my own nerves had mercifully steadied, as they usually do, with action. But now they were returning, and in greater force than mere sympathy to her own fears could explain.

My own eyes began traveling as I spoke. "Well? Do I get some answers?"

"You know as much as you need to," she replied mechanically. "You will be duly informed of *what* is necessary, *when* it is necessary, and not before. In the meantime, you are to keep your questions to yourself, Mr. McDaniel."

"Ducky," I sighed.

For the moment, it seemed best to lighten up. In spite of my earlier boast, it was definitely important to gain this woman's friendship. Without it, getting answers would have to become a gruesome prospect, and she was just too vulnerable and pretty for that.

I allowed some warmth into my voice. "I'd ask one thing of you, if I might."

She relaxed the slightest bit. "What would that be?"

"Call me Liam," I smiled. "You see, my father had to be one of the stuffiest bastards that ever crawled off a potato farm. He got himself a fancy education in Dublin, and became headmaster at a little school in Warwick. And from that day on, he wouldn't allow for anyone, not even his own children, to call him anything but *Mr. McDaniel!* It kind of stiffens my bowels every time I hear it."

A hint of a smile crept across her face, and I transferred my own gaze out into the street for fear of chasing it off.

And that's when I spotted him.

"All right . . . Liam," she sighed. "I imagine I can

grant you that much.''

I turned back to her, my grin firmly in place, but my voice hoarse with tension. ''Keep talking!''

''What?'' she stammered, confusion now replacing the glimmer of amusement.

I laughed out loud before repeating myself. ''I said keep talking, about anything! Just keep talking, and keep smiling.''

It took a second, but finally she obeyed. She began a line of chatter about this being her first visit to Algiers, and what she had been doing with her time. I kept up a veneer of smiles and you-don't-says, but my mind was nowhere near her conversation.

I had already spotted the man on the far corner, and now I had to try to determine if he was solo, or if he had company. Each mechanical response to her talking took my eyes in another direction, until I had covered the entire street and café.

There were two of them, at least in sight. The one against the building on the far corner, and the other two tables away, near the entry door to the inner part of the café.

And now I had the answer to my question: 'Why have my jitters returned?' It had nothing to do with her. There is something unique about being a survivor in the ''spook '' business. You learn to use your guts almost as much as your eyes and ears. You can almost feel an enemy near you.

And you can almost always smell a KGB man.

That the two of them were KGB was beyond doubt. There is a drab, humorless rigidity to them that defies disguise or concealment. There is a grayness to them that covers them like a tan covers a native islander. It's hereditary. Conjure in your mind one image of the

U.S.S.R., one single landscape or cityscape that you feel most typifies the place.

I'll give you ten-to-one odds, the sun isn't shining.

I now knew they were there, and I knew who they were, but I still had to determine why. I knew for a fact they hadn't been tailing me, so that only left the madonna. I was relatively certain she was an amateur, and they make easy targets for professional shadows. The only other option was that they were the lady's playmates.

"Keep smiling, Robin," I said. "It seems we have company."

"What!" Her head started to move.

"Don't look," I hissed. "Just answer me. Are they friends of yours?"

"Certainly not!" Her vehemence and surprise were genuine beyond a doubt.

"Well, they seem to have followed you here, and it looks as though we'll have to lose them, wouldn't you say?"

Fear was creeping back into her eyes. "How?" she asked.

"First of all, relax. Keep smiling, and then excuse yourself. There is bound to be a bathroom inside, and you're suddenly going to need it. And don't be afraid to let the tables near us hear about it."

The smile jumped back onto her face. "And just what the hell am I going to do in the bathroom?"

"Nothing, my dear girl. Once you get inside, you are going to find us a back door. If there is one, you send out the waiter and wait for me. If there isn't one, you'll just have to stall a bit, toss on some powder, and come back out looking about one liter more relieved. We'll devise another ploy if necessary."

She did as she was told, and disappeared into the café.

I watched the goon at the table, and he did nothing. Quickly I checked the street. Goon number two was not as cooperative. He immediately made a beeline across the street and around to where he could check the back of the building.

It was beginning to look like a little rough stuff would become necessary. I was definitely prepared. My three dearest friends were with me. Wilhelmina, my 9mm Luger, was tucked comfortably under my jacket; Hugo, my pencil-thin stiletto, was nestled in its chamois case and hugging the right forearm beneath my shirt; and Pierre, a tiny but very lethal gas bomb, was in its usual position as the third member in the Carter family jewels.

Suddenly I heard McDaniel's name called, and turned to see the waiter standing in the doorway. He called out to me that there was a phone call, and I thanked him. I took a quick swallow of tea in order to give the waiter time to vanish.

Robin had done her job well.

Having watched his buddy disappear with Robin's departure, I was sure the goon at the table would not let me out of his sight. He would have to be neutralized.

I had no idea of how proficient either of them was with his hands, but at least I could test them out one at a time.

I also had surprise on my side. I knew they were blown, and they didn't. Goon number two would most assuredly spot us out back, but I was sure I could either shake him, or take him. The first chore was to retire number one.

I got up and began making my way toward the café's interior, making damn sure I walked right past my mark. About two steps away, I faked a stumble, driving into him, and pounding him gently on the back of the neck with the side of my hand.

A one-way ticket to dreamland.

His body slumped and his head hit the table. I gave a quick look around. Nobody had noticed it. To keep it that way, I reached over and borrowed an empty bottle from a nearby table. I placed it in front of him, right next to his half-empty glass.

I was sure he would be left quite alone to sleep off his apparent drunk.

I quickly moved inside, and spotted Robin back in a corner around the bar. The atmosphere inside was dark and smoky, but I fought the stinging in my eyes, and checked the interior for reinforcements. The place looked clean.

I joined Robin, following her down a narrow passage that smelled like one thousand years worth of falafel. She showed me the door, and I motioned her to wait.

Slowly I eased it open. I found myself looking out into a narrow alleyway. Everything in the direction of the opening looked clear. I then turned back and glanced through the crack on the hinged side of the door.

Number two goon reporting for duty, sir!

I returned to Robin. "All right," I whispered. "One of our playmates is still with us. With any luck, his orders are just to follow, and I'm sure we can shake him. If things do start getting rough, I want you to hit the ground and stay there until further notice. Got that?"

She nodded. "What about the other one?"

"Sleeping quite peacefully, thank you."

She grabbed my arm with a strength that startled me. "Is he dead?" she gasped.

I gently loosened her grip. "No, but he'll have one hell of a headache when he wakes up."

Relief poured over her.

"Shall we?" I said, and took her arm as we moved out through the door.

We made directly for the clear end of the alley. I kept my eyes intent on the opening before me, but I tuned my ears in behind. Number two was on us, and he wasn't being subtle any more. His pace was picking up rapidly. The sound of his footsteps were being joined by a second, and along with it, the crackle of static that told me someone had a radio communicator.

It was obviously going to become necessary to break heads.

I released my grip on Robin, and turned to face my pursuers. There were indeed two of them, and much to my surprise they came to a dead stop when faced. The reason why became immediately apparent.

From behind me I could hear the squeal of tires. I turned back around, and caught sight of a dark blue Citröen. It had nosed itself into the alley, blocking any hope of escape in that direction. The driver was the first to pile out, but it was the second man in the car, the one on the passenger side, that got my attention. His exit was much slower, but then he had his hands full.

I bet myself eight to five he was a Russian. There was just no mistaking a Kalishnikov AK47.

CHAPTER FOUR

There were two possibilities. Either they would take us alive, or we'd be fertilizing an oasis somewhere south of Algiers.

I decided the worst, and made the guy with the Kalishnikov my first concern.

"Robin?" The word slid quietly out of the corner of my mouth. There was no response. "Goddammit, Robin! Don't disappear on me now!"

I was relieved to hear a whispered return. "I'm still here."

She was frightened, but the voice was steady enough to give me hope.

"You've got to do me a favor, *luvy*." It worked. On the word "luvy", she shot me a look. If she could still be pissed about that, she was still in the game.

I continued. "Sooner or later they're going to want to take us for a ride. Personally, I'd rather not go. So I'm going to have to persuade the chap with the rifle—"

That was as far as I got. I felt a pair of hands pound into my back, propelling me toward the Citröen. Robin joined me, her motivation for doing so no less gentle than my own.

"Oh, my God!" Robin's voice was beginning to whimper. I could not afford to lose her now.

Fortunately, our escorts were maintaining a safe distance behind.

"Stay with me, damnit. I just need a second or two,

that's all. Do something . . . anything . . . but get their attention for a few seconds.''

"But . . . *what?*'' The cracking in her voice was making me feel anything but confident.

I never got a chance to answer. The hands behind me returned, propelling me the final two or three feet to the front of the car. Just as quickly, I was spread across the hood and searched. Wilhelmina was removed instantly. I had never expected to be able to hang on to my gun, but I was hoping that whoever claimed it would tuck it away.

No such luck.

It remained in the man's hands, quite ready to use. That would have to be my second object of concern.

Pierre was out of the question. A gas bomb allowed too many seconds for reaction, was too awkward to get at. Also, it could just as easily take Robin and myself with it.

It become vital that I hold onto my stiletto, Hugo.

The first man, having found my gun, had moved backward to cover me, while the Citröen's driver finished the search. Before the driver could reach my forearm, I drew my right hand into a fist and flexed every tendon and sinew in my arm.

I held my breath.

The beauty of Hugo's design is that he is pencil thin. He is mounted with two objectives in mind. First, to rest very carefully between the large tendons of my right wrist and forearm, and thereby disappear when they are tensed. Secondly, with the appropriate angling of my wrist and the gentlest nudge of hip or third object, he will slip quietly and quickly into my waiting palm.

I was tensing for all I was worth, and to my great relief the driver passed right over Hugo.

Hurdle one had been cleared.

Now I needed my diversion. The driver stepped away from me and I rose up from the hood. I turned to face Robin, carefully measuring the distance between myself and the Kalishnikov as I did so. She was being searched by the jerk who had been tailing her. He had just completed a quick survey of her purse and was in the process of tossing it to the Citröen's driver, when I turned.

The driver held onto it.

I made a quick mental thank-you to both men. At least one pair of hands would be occupied when I went into action.

That is, *if* I went into action.

My quick perusal of Robin left me less optimistic. The man searching her was spending far more time on it than he had to. The leer on his face was anything but subtle as he gave the areas beneath her skirt a far too thorough examination. She was beginning to crack. Tears welled in her eyes and her cheeks were quivering visibly.

I threw my mental radio into high gear, and silently screamed for her attention.

The amateur telepathy must have worked, because I got it. Her eyes jumped over to mine, just as the man began working his way up the outside of her blouse. I nodded ever so slightly, hoping she would understand that now was the time to move.

Her eyes closed tightly, and tears began to spill as the searcher cupped her right breast. His gesture was accompanied by guttural grunts of laughter from all the onlookers.

I gave Kalishnikov a quick look. He had stepped back, ever so slightly, He had his eyes riveted on me.

All my chips were on Robin. It had to be now, with Ivan's hands all over her tits.

Then, suddenly, she moved. Ivan was just getting ready to make his considered appraisal of her left breast, when she hauled off and slapped him. The shock of her blow, more than the power, sent him back about two steps.

I used the moment to begin a careful inching toward the rifle. My mental broadcasts were still on full charge. *Good girl, keep it up. Keep it up!*

The surprised look on Ivan's face gave way to a slow smile. He moved back to her, a study in gestured forgiveness. But no sooner had he reached her, than he let go with a slap of his own.

It shook her to the bone. She rocked back on her heels, while I inched one more step toward my target, praying that she wouldn't let down now, that she would stay mad.

She hauled off and belted him again.

Good girl! I had gained another inch.

There was no delay this time, no smiling façade before contact. With a fury that made my heart skip, the Russian slammed her again, then grabbed her upper arms with a force that should have broken them and sent her sailing against the far wall of the alley. Her head bounced sickeningly off the white stucco.

And still he continued. He caught her on the rebound and sent his palm twice more into the soft flesh of her cheeks. Finally his honor seemed satisfied. He stepped back slowly and awaited what could only be her inevitable collapse.

The bout had provided me with my final two inches, and Hugo was now nestled securely in my palm.

My right hand sailed out, and released Hugo. There was no room for error, and Hugo came through like a trouper. He found his way into Kalishnikov's neck and sailed clean through, severing the windpipe as he went.

A look of horrified shock spread across the man's face. My left hand came over and grabbed the rifle. I gave it a hard jerk, but there was no resistance. His body had already surrendered to the numbing reality of death.

It was time to move on.

My second concern was the goon holding Wilhelmina. Moving targets make for difficult aiming, so I danced off to my left, pulling the Kalishnikov into firing position as I went. My back slammed into the alley wall, bringing me to a halt. There wasn't enough time, with four men to deal with, to allow myself the luxury of careful aim. So I merely began blasting away in the general direction of my target.

No contest.

To the man's credit, he had managed to get Wilhelmina up to operating level, but the first of my volleys cut him in half like a weed.

There were two choices left, and I had little time to think. Instinct carried me instantly toward the man who had battered Robin. On the one hand, there was an incredible desire on my part to return the treatment in kind he had given her; and on the other hand, I was still operating on my previous observation that the driver's hands were busy holding Robin's purse.

By the time I faced number three, he was already digging into his coat for his gun. Another burst from the Kalishnikov sent him sprawling backwards, the bullets nailing his hands to the inside of his jacket.

As he fell, I mentally blessed Robin. Not only had she given me the diversion I needed to act, but she had gotten herself down and out of the way, all at the same time. I would have to thank her. But that was for later.

Still one to go.

I turned for the finale, but the driver, by now, had

been given too much time. I had pinned my hopes on Robin's purse slowing him down, and now I would pay for it. Number four was just a cut above his buddies.

By the time I turned to greet him, there was no scramble. He was waiting for me, and he was moving. Unfortunately I only caught the merest glimpse of it because the next thing I saw was Robin's purse hitting me square in the middle of my face.

I fired blindly, hoping to get lucky. But luck had run out. A well-placed foot smashed into the back of my hand, sending the Kalishnikov flying. While my other hand tore the purse away, there came a second foot, equally as well-placed, driving itself into the middle of my body.

I hit the ground with a force that was less than comfortable. Whatever tiny amount of air that had remained in my lungs was gone, on contact. A tiny voice in the back of my head was screaming for me to move, but my body just couldn't cooperate. I lay on the ground, fighting for air, and did my best to raise myself up, but my best only got me as far as my elbows.

By then, it was too late anyway.

While my mind was screaming, his was operating. By the time I had gasped the first soothing intakes of oxygen, I was staring into the muzzle of his gun. The moment seemed to stretch itself out for an eternity. While I struggled to regain a regular pattern of breathing, he just smiled, awaiting the sadistically ripe moment when he could bring my efforts to their point-less demise.

The gun cracked.

My eyes clamped shut and my face twisted into a grimace as I awaited the burning surge of pain that would transport Nick Carter into immortality.

It didn't come.

I reopened my eyes and watched the driver collapse, a giant beret of red where the left side of his skull used to reside.

That was my first surprise.

The second was to flip myself over and see Robin, Wilhelmina still smoking in her hands, lowering the gun and staring in horror at what she had just accomplished.

I made a mental note to myself. Never underestimate the creativity and courage of an amateur, particularly when his life is threatened.

The gun slipped from her hand as she continued staring blankly at where her target had once stood. I rose up quickly and retrieved Wilhelmina, then moved to where Robin stood. The gunfire was bound to have gotten someone's attention, and a hasty retreat was definitely in order. The last thing I needed was for Robin to panic.

I was now standing directly before her, but her eyes were boring clear through me, intent on the memory of the driver's death at her own hands. Her breathing was becoming labored, and the echo of a cry was working its way into her throat.

My first impulse was to slap her, but the visible signs of her previous battering dissuaded me. A rather novel idea struck me. If violence was what was setting her off, perhaps gentleness would be shock enough to bring her out of it.

On impulse I held her face, and pressed my lips onto hers.

They were hard and unyielding, but I pressed on for several seconds. Finally I released her. She stepped back a pace, and caught her breath. Her eyes blinked open and closed a few times, then finally focused clearly on mine.

"Sorry," she whispered.

I breathed a sigh of relief. "Good girl. You were wonderful. Now I need you to do only one thing. Go to the car, pack yourself neatly into the passenger seat, and just sit. Do you understand me?"

She nodded. "I'll let you know if the keys are in it."

She was thinking; a very good sign. "Excellent," I grinned, stroking her face in gratitude. "Now scoot, we haven't much time!"

She was gone in an instant.

As quickly as I could, I searched each of the four men, retrieving Robin's purse and Hugo in the process. With the exception of two matchbooks, the search yielded nothing out of the ordinary. The matchbooks themselves might not have created interest, were it not for the fact that they were both the same, yet each had come from the pockets of two different men.

They were lettered in Arabic, and I was struggling to make sense of the scrolling, when Robin's voice reached me.

"They keys are in it. I think I hear sirens!"

She was right; the sirens were distant but approaching. I pocketed the two matchbooks and raced to my position behind the wheel. The car started instantly, and I gunned it back out of the alley. With the first jarring surge of movement, Robin's eyes closed again, but all else remained composed.

I slammed into first and charged off, not slackening speed until the relative anonymity of one of the larger boulevards had been reached. Then I maneuvered the car into the normal flow of traffic.

Only then did Robin's eyes reopen.

Once on the road, my mind filled with questions. I, as Liam MacDaniel, was obviously not working for the Russians. Then, who was I working for? And who was I supposed to kill; and why; and where?

I looked over at Robin. She was staring out the

window, clutching at her blouse to keep it closed. She appeared normal, but the slackness of her body and the blank look in her eyes told me that she was numb. She was in shock. Interrogations were obviously better left for a later time.

There was one matter, however, that could not be tucked on the shelf. I was forced to break the silence.

"I owe you my life. I know what you did back there was difficult, and I wish there were some way I could make it seem like it all makes sense. But I can't. I'm just grateful you did it."

Silence.

"Look, Robin, I know the best friend you've got right now is your solitude. But there is one thing we've got to talk through."

Still no response.

I sighed and continued. "We've been blown, my love. You've been tailed, I've been spotted, and somebody seems to want both of us as guest of honor at a grave digging. Your hotel is no doubt under surveillance, your room has no doubt been searched, your plane reservations, no doubt duly noted. And for all I know, everything in the envelope you gave me is, right now, being swapped for gossip by every housewife, over every picket fence in North Africa."

Finally she stirred. "What should we do?"

I logged a 'thank God' into the mental books.

"In the first place, we're going to have to find alternate lodging. Any suggestions?"

She shrugged. "I've never been here before."

"Ducky," I groaned.

"Wait a minute," she added. "But I do know someone! An Arab girl. She was an exchange student in Johannesburg. She was from Algiers."

"What was her name?"

There was a moment's pause for thought. "Adjana! Adjana Mousif!"

I began searching the street for any place that looked like it would hold a phone book.

"Let's just hope she never got married," I muttered.

"Why? You interested in her?" Her question was followed by a burst of giggles.

I just glared at her before asking, "Is she about your size?"

Another burst of giggles. "My, you are interested, aren't you!"

The human psyche has many ways of dealing with extreme tension. Her giggling was beginning to worry me as much as her silence.

"Look," I said, as evenly as I could. "You can't go back to your hotel, and you're going to need fresh clothing. That is, unless you want to dilate every pupil between here and South Africa."

She flashed a quick look down to her blouse. "Yes. She is about my size . . . or was, at any rate."

"Good. Now, is there anything back at your hotel that you can't afford to give up?"

She thought a moment. "Just one thing that I can recall."

"What?"

She barely got it out. "My douche bag," and the giggles were back in full force.

I let it go as long as I could stand it. "You know something?" I said, "I think I liked you much more when you were morose."

The giggling subsided and she turned to glare first at me and then out the window. It was about this time that I spotted a phone stall and pulled over. "Let's see if Mademoiselle Mousif is listed!"

Just before she got out, she turned and looked at me

for a moment. "She hasn't gotten married," she said. "And it wouldn't pay to be interested." There was a slight pause, and then a wide grin split her beautiful face. "She's gay!" she chirped, and with that she departed for the phone.

I merely shook my head as I stared after her. And then I remembered the matchbooks.

I took them out and studied them once more, but no matter how hard I tried, I could not make out the characters of the lettering. It was just so many delicate, Arabic sweeps over cardboard.

I reached over and opened the glove compartment. I was in luck. A map of Algiers lay tucked in the bottom. I pulled it out, and began scanning the street. A quick glance at Robin found her dialing the phone. A good sign. Meanwhile, my rearview mirror filled with the light of an approaching bicycle, complete with Arab rider. *Allah be praised*.

I leaned out the window and flagged him down. His English was poor, but good enough to communicate. I showed him the matchbooks. "Can you tell me where these are from?"

His black eyes twinkled and his throat erupted in a hearty chuckle as he looked at the logo on the cover. *"Oui, oui, monsieur*, I know of it!'' he cackled. "It is The Bakery of Heavenly Delights!"

"The Bakery of Heavenly Delights?" Surely he was kidding.

"Oui . . . a very special place, *monsieur*. You would like it!'' He was nearly falling off his bicycle in his merriment.

I asked him to show me where it was, and he did so, his helpful finger tracing out a path on my map. I thanked him and sent him on his way a few dinar richer, his shoulders still twitching with laughter as he peddled away, waving his *adieus*.

The Bakery of Heavenly Delights.

Surely, I was once more in luck. If the matches had read Café or Night Club or Bath House. I might have been convinced to scrap them. These are places one makes a special effort to travel to, across town if necessary, because they appeal to specific tastes or needs or interests.

The Bakery of Heavenly Delights.

One does not usually travel across town for a donut, or for coffee, and two never do. Two drop next door for those items, and it was my sincerest hope that that was what our twin friends had done. I had an outside chance of locating the enemy.

And I intended to follow it through.

The matches found their way back into my pocket, just as Robin was piling back into the car.

"She's only about a mile from here," she said. "And she's thrilled to death to give us roof and robing."

Her spirits were obviously elevated.

"Jolly good show," I breathed, and pulled the car back out into the mainstream of traffic.

"Liam?"

"Yes?"

There was a pause. "I'll need to contact my people. Alternative plans and all."

I gave no reply.

"I'll need to do it alone."

I looked over and smiled. "No trouble, my love. I have a few errands of my own to run. Unlike your lovely self, my belongings are currently residing at the American Express office. It shouldn't be too much risk for me to claim them."

A more relaxed silence carried us the mile to our

destination. I stopped the car, and waited for Robin to exit. She crawled out, but paused and leaned back in through the open window.

"Liam . . . be careful." Her face was almost childlike as she spoke.

"Does it really matter?"

She froze, then turned and moved toward the tiny house.

I remembered I owed her. "Robin!"

She turned and halted.

"Thanks. You, too."

She smiled, then disappeared through the door.

It was time to gather my bearings, and time to pay a visit. Robin would make her call in peace and secrecy, I would retrieve a clean shirt and toothbrush from American Express, and, in the meantime, try to locate the particular pile of camel dung from which our four gadflies had arisen.

CHAPTER FIVE

The Bakery of Heavenly Delights turned out to be a dive, a whorehouse, with a powdered sugar and honey façade.

It was located a few blocks from the wharf section of town. The smell of the Mediterranean scented the air like perfume. I had taken up surveillance from an alleyway directly across, and it hadn't taken me long to figure out how the place worked.

Within the space of one hour, I had watched three merchant seamen, two Italians, and one Turk and numerous locals enter the establishment and receive a room key. They would then exit and move down to the next doorway. It was a weathered wooden slab, perpetually open, long ago torn from its ancient hinges. Through this opening I could watch the men climb a rickety flight of steps to the second floor, where I was certain they would match key to door, and await their pleasures.

Seconds after they would disappear, the bakery door would open and out would step one of those "heavenly delights" the bakery was so proud of producing. In minutes she would join her newfound confection-lover in his upstairs abode.

I observed that the bakery had a varied inventory, indeed: chocolate and vanilla, thick tarts with lots of stuffing, and slim, delicate ladyfingers, old goods that had been on the shelf for years, and freshly baked buns, barely out of the oven. In the latter category were two

ladies that might have matched twenty-one years between them.

There had even been one boy; adolescent, and beautiful, but with the eyes of a war-weary soldier.

I found myself cursing my luck. Kismet had failed
me again. My two Russian buddies would do little more
than cross the street for the "Bakery" end of the business, but for the "Heavenly Delights" they would be
willing to cross the globe for all I knew.

I was about to write the whole project off as a source
for any clues, when Kismet suddenly seemed to jump
back on my side.

A man entered the bakery. I hadn't really gotten a
good look at his face yet, but his bearing and manner
made him completely out of place. There was nothing
about him that fit. He didn't display the over-anxious
eagerness from months at sea, nor did he carry the dust
of a long, lonely caravan that would bring him to this
particular oasis.

His dress was simple enough: plain brown slacks,
and a sports coat, with a simple turtleneck sweater
beneath. Nothing exceptional in itself, except that he
didn't look at home in his own clothes. His posture and
carriage spoke of suits—years of them—and the best
money could buy. His clothing was humble, but the
body beneath was arrogant; too used to giving orders to
bend to the will of a few threads of cotton.

It wasn't until he had re-entered the street, his key in
hand, that I understood why.

I had only seen a few pictures of the man, and never
one that was recent. It was probably *that* fact that
enabled me to recognize him. I knew his age to be
around forty-seven, but he was trying to pass for ten
years younger. His salt-and-pepper hair was dyed
blonde, but the overall effect was that of a great shock

of silver. On his face was a pair of wire-rimmed glasses that did little to hide the icy coldness behind those eyes.

Suits were definitely this man's normal armor, and power his usual sword; the kind of absolute power you can only get in a Communist state.

I was staring at Yuri Berenko himself, next in line to run the KGB.

I watched him vanish up the stairs, and waited to see who would be joining him. Whoever it was, they wouldn't be casual. Berenko was no dabbler; he didn't have to be. If Berenko wanted diversion, he could *order* it, courtesy of Moscow, and á la carte. He didn't need to creep around the backstreets of Algiers to find it.

My suspicions were quickly confirmed.

Out from the bakery stepped a most atypical "delight." She was black, and incredibly beautiful. She wore a multicolored dashiki that seemed to swallow up her birdlike body. Her face was carved in ebony, a study in arrogant defiance, and topped by a native hairdo, generously laced with colorful beads.

She was an African princess, plucked from the lush gardens of the rain forest, and as much at home in this North African strip of sand as a pearl in a pigpen.

I watched her follow the yellow brick road up to the waiting Berenko, her walk measured and haughty. No sister of the night, this one. Definitely a class act.

I waited a few minutes more to see if anyone else would join the party, but no one arrived. I held myself in check for a moment, trying to make sense of what *appeared* to be the most outrageous of fortunes.

Berenko would no more wander the streets unescorted than would the President himself. There had to be watchdogs somewhere. And yet the street was an empty as a cutthroat's soul.

I made a quick mental review of all who had entered,

searching for details I might have previously over-looked.

Nope. There was nothing in the replay to give me any indication that the previous occupants were anything but what they seemed.

Berenko was solo, except for the girl. At least from the outside. Inside might be a different story, but if there were any rats hiding in the rafters, they were on to Robin, not me. The only goon who would know my face would be the slob I had put to sleep in the café.

I would just have to hope that he was still napping.

This was too golden a prospect to ignore. I needed to know why the Russians were tailing Robin, and what their intentions were in general. I saw no reason not to go straight to the top. If there was information to be had, no one would have it like Berenko.

I moved out into the street and made my way toward the open door. I moved as casually as my pumping heart would allow, my ears tuned to the first hint of a *"Nyet!"*; but none was forthcoming.

I entered the door and paused. Still nothing. I removed Wilhelmina from her home inside my coat and started climbing up the stairs. There was an occasional groan of age as my feet hit certain of the ancient steps, but I ignored them. Those treads were too used to constant traffic, as were the people who preceded me, to worry about silence.

I made the second level, and checked out the corridor. It was all doors, both left and right, and nary a Commie in sight. I sighed in relief.

And then I muttered a silent oath.

Things were just too easy. Having fate on one's side was one thing; having her ready to hop into bed with you was another. I always get just a little frightened when events move too smoothly.

I waited a few minutes longer, but in spite of my longings, chaos simply refused to rear her ugly head.

I moved cautiously into the hall, stepping from door to door, listening for the telltale signs that would locate Berenko. I heard groans, and gasps, the gentle strains of leather on flesh, the bored drone of a young boy's voice, the light taunting of the adolescent girls who had already lost the laughter of their youth.

And then I found them; calm and conversational, the only intercourse being short bursts of German as they talked over the fate of the world. The door was just a little too thick for me to pick up more than a word or two at a time, so I opted for entry. Cautiously I tested the latch, fully expecting it to be locked.

Fate was not only in the sack; she was hot to trot, and on the pill!

I burst through the door and slammed it behind me. I threw my back to the wall, my feet dancing left and right, while Wilhelmina searched the room for response.

All I got for my efforts was the astonished stares of Berenko and his lady. They were sitting on the bed, fully clothed, and embracing no more than their individual reasons for being there.

I centered Wilhelmina square between Berenko's eyes.

"Bring them out, *now!*" I barked.

The two looked at each other blankly.

"Bring who out?" said Berenko.

At the moment, I wasn't even sure myself. The room was devoid of reinforcements, with four blank walls, and not even a closet to break the monotony. There were, however, two large windows.

The buildings was of typical Mediterranean design; huge and square, with a central open courtyard. Across this court, I could see the windows of the rest of the building.

If Berenko did have company, they would no doubt be occupying one of those overlooking rooms, and would have done so long before the hour had begun when I took up my vigil.

"Both of you," I snapped, using Wilhelmina for emphasis, "up against those windows. Take one each, face it, *fill it,* and keep your hands up in plain sight. Now!"

Berenko was the only one to rise. The girl merely stared at me. I gave her a clear view down Wilhelmina's barrel. "Move!" I shouted.

Quietly, Berenko repeated my instructions to the girl, in German. She nodded, stood, and moved into the right-hand window, while Berenko filled the left.

The pointed way in which the verbal exchange was done was not lost on me.

I approached the two, feeling relatively secure that no one across the court would take any pot shots with the boss in the way.

I gave them a quick search for arms. I liberated Berenko's Walther and tucked it into my coat pocket. The girl was clean. Satisfied that I was the only one carrying persuasion, I drifted off to my left and placed my back against the wall containing the windows.

"Okay, back to the bed, both of you!"

Berenko turned and escorted the black beauty back to their original positions on the bed, while I gave the wall behind me a quick scan.

To my right and slightly above me, stood a huge crack in the wall heavily stained by time, or whatever particular delight had struck the fancy of some prior occupant.

I turned back to my roommates.

The eyes of both of them were studying me, hers in cold appraisal, his in rapt concentration.

"See this?" I allowed my head to gesture toward the wall's blemished surface. "I want both of you to stare at it. No matter what I do, or where I go, I want both of you to study nothing else but this crack. Am I being sufficiently clear?"

Berenko, once more, repeated the instructions in German.

While he was doing so, I slid my back down the wall and inched my way, well below sill level, to the other side of the two windows. Then I climbed back up to a standing position in the corner behind the two, and covered them.

More specifically, I was covering my own ass. If Berenko had help, and if that help was occupying one of those neighboring windows, they now knew I was here, and not in a friendly mood. Being unable to nail me through the windows, they would no doubt be hell-bent for the door.

But not without guidance.

Someone would have to remain at that window to give them their bearings. And, at the moment, the guy at that window would be studying the eyes of my two companions, trying to pin down my location. Whenever the gorillas at the door were ready, they would come in blasting.

My hope was that they would be directed toward the crack that Berenko and his girl were staring at.

I waited for the sounds of action.

Two minutes must have passed before Berenko broke the silence. He spoke in clear, accented English.

"Sorry to disappoint you, my good friend, but I and the lady are . . . or, rather, *were* . . . disturbingly alone."

I remained silent merely awaiting the inevitable.
There was no way I was going to give them a voice to
fix in on.

Two more minutes passed.

Again Berenko spoke. "There are no reinforcements, my friend. Your caution, not to mention your
skills, are both admirable. But we do seem to be wast-
ing precious moments in a ridiculous limbo, when our
time would be better spent in sorting out this little
misunderstanding. Do you not agree?"

There was an irritating half-smile on his face as he
awaited my reply. What was even more irritating was
the growing possibility that he was telling the truth.

"I would love to believe you," I finally muttered,
sotto voce, "but somehow I just can't accept the idea of
Yuri Berenko wandering around in the rain without an
umbrella or two."

In spite of the expressed emphasis of my earlier
demand that all eyes remain on the wall, the princess
broke her gaze and shot Berneko a dark stare. I cor-
rected the situation quickly.

"Drop your eyes from that wall one more time,
darling, and you'll be wearing two new beads in your
hair, both of them solid lead!"

In total defiance, she turned and stared at me. My
finger instinctively tightened on the trigger, but the
panicked urgency in Berenko's voice halted the final
squeeze.

"You fool! She doesn't speak English!"

I had already gleaned as much, but Berenko didn't
have to know that. By feigning ignorance of the language, I could achieve two things. The first had just
been accomplished: complicate the flow of communi-
cation, and keep Berenko on edge and off guard. The
second advantage would reveal itself as time went on.
If the two of them decided to tell secrets, they would do

so in German. I would then be able to eavesdrop.

"Tell her to watch the wall, Berenko!"

He glared at me for a moment, and then heaved a giant sigh, the kind of sigh a father gives his son when the boy has misspent his allowance.

"Tell her yourself, Mr. Carter. You know the language as well as I!"

So he knew me! For some odd reason I was flattered. Oh, well, so much for subtlety. Round one to Berenko.

I turned to the girl and began expounding in Teutonic elegance, "Either watch the wall, *fraulein*, or I'll be forced to turn your lovely face into bratwurst!"

She obeyed, but not before removing my innards with her eyes. And those eyes were two bullets, right out of the freezer.

I looked at Berenko. At the first sound of German from me, the smug little half-smile had returned to his lips. I had to do something about that; I had to get him rattled. Berenko had been in the business far too long for me to assume he would cough up any real information. The only way he was going to tell me anything was by letting his emotions register, and in order for that to happen, I would have to loosen his grip on them.

I gambled first on the possibility that he wasn't using his own name in his dealings with the girl. I spoke in German, so she would understand exactly what was going on.

"Now, tell me. What is it that brings the great Yuri Berenko to Africa?"

For a moment the smile collapsed, but then it returned in force.

"Ahhhh," he sighed, his own German ringing out. "I thought as much. A simple error, my friend. You mistake me for somebody else. The name is Schmidt, Einar Schmidt."

I laughed. *"Ja, und ich bin Whistler's Mother!"*

His jaw tightened and his eyes shot to the girl to measure her responses. She sat immobile, her eyes glued to the wall. I didn't check, but I knew that wherever her gaze was falling, there was now a thick coating of frost.

Finally he spoke, but this time in English. "You're a very rude man, Mr. Carter!"

"So slap my wrists."

The smile was gone. "Someday I will, Mr. Carter. *That* I promise you."

The girl moved. I brought my gun over to cover her, but false alarm. She crossed her arms and began toying with the beads in her hair, her boredom evident to both of us.

I returned my eyes to Berenko, dissecting every movement and glimmer of response in his face.

"Talk to me, *Herr* Schmidt." My voice was not without sarcasm. "I get lonely when I'm ignored."

Hate registered in his eyes. "I'm afraid there is little to discuss," he said. "Perhaps a responsive reading would amuse you. There must be a Bible in the hotel somewhere."

"Well, if you won't talk to me, perhaps the girl will. I'm sure she'd just love to know the credentials of her bedmate."

I could swear that for just one second, his eyes grew harder than the glasses that covered them.

"Just what is it you wish to know, Mr. Carter?"

"First of all, who's the raven?" I asked.

"An interesting question," he spat. "One I might have been able to answer, had we not been so abruptly interrupted."

I let it slide.

"And what brings you to Africa?"

"The climate, Mr. Carter. I'm looking for a nice condominium to retire to."

Before I could respond, a small rumble of voices exploded in the hall. I tensed, studying Berenko. He was as surprised as I. Apparently, one of the customers had had his fill, and was leaving. High-pitched voices told me the two young girls had finished dispensing their "heavenly delights". The sounds drifted down the stairs, and I eased up on Wilhelmina.

We were getting nowhere, fast.

"I think maybe we should take a ride, Berenko. This place is a little too crowded for my tastes. And we have so much to chat over."

"I doubt that," he replied coldly.

"We'll see. The car is about one block from here. You'll drive. The raven and I will watch from the back seat. It shouldn't present any difficulties for you. After all, it's one of your cars!"

His eyes widened.

"Oh, that's right," I added, "I forgot to tell you. Your buddies won't be home for supper tonight. Four of them, at any rate. The fifth will, but he'll have one hell of a headache. The other four will make interesting rugs for the fireplace."

His eyes leaped up to my face. If I didn't know better, I could swear he didn't know what the hell I was talking about.

"And by the way," I continued, my own expression smug and gloating, "you really should convince your children not to play with matches. A quick dive through their pockets led me straight to you."

His look baffled me. Anger I could live with; hate, I expected. But all I got was blankness; stark, unknowing, questioning, *confusion*.

And then I received something else.

My eyes had been so intent on Berenko that I almost failed to catch her movement. It was brief and economical, nothing one would leap to catch.

But movement it was, nonetheless.

With a quick jerk of her hand, she tore one of the beads from her hair and threw it at me. I moved instinctively, allowing the wooden ball to hit me on the right forearm and fall away.

But it never fell.

Attached to the end of it was a tiny needle, that now penetrated my arm, numbing the surrounding nerves in the process. In surprise, my trigger finger tensed, waking Wilhelmina into action. The shot went wild and slammed into the wall.

At that instant, both of them moved. She dove forward onto the floor, while Berenko slid off the bed and rolled toward the door. I shook my right arm as hard as I could, and the bead fell out. I returned my hand to the trigger, ready to obliterate the first one that moved.

Berenko had torn open the door, and the black girl was now making her dash for it. Given my choice of targets, I leveled my aim on the man who was destined to become the head of one of the deadliest organizations in the world.

My finger tensed on the trigger, intent on releasing him from his earthly burdens.

No response.

My mind was screaming "Pull!", but the finger refused to obey. The earlier sensation in my arm, cool and numbing, was now growing into a full brushfire of agonizing pain. No message, no matter how intensely sent, was capable of getting from brain to finger without burning to a crisp.

And the fire was spreading, moving up my arm, hungry for the chance to reach my skull and bake it. The alarms went off like skyrockets.

Poison. Goddamnit, *poison!*

The sound of my gun had alerted the entire floor to trouble. A tornado of activity whipped itself up in the hall. I was helpless to stop Berenko as he joined the anonymous masses, his own voice loudest in his questioning panic. "What was that? Where did it come from? My god, my wife will find out. I've got to get out of here!"

I had to move fast.

My left arm was still with me, responding to every command in faithful obedience. I dropped Wilhelmina, and, with my left hand, I jammed up the sleeve of my coat, ripping open my shirt sleeve at the same time. I then tore at the casing that held my stiletto, successfully releasing it, and slashed Hugo over the point the dart had entered.

There was nothing sophisticated about the incision, but then, scars I could live with. If I lived.

Hugo's blade ripped open my arm, and I lowered my lips to the cut, sucking at the poison for all I was worth. For what seemed an eternity, I did my damnedest to stop the progress of pain up my arm. Fanatically I dedicated myself to the task of living, and finally an impasse was reached.

The pain seemed to halt, somewhere about mid-shoulder.

As I consumed the last few platelets of my own blood and spit them onto the floor, other thoughts triggered through my fogging brain.

I could still hear Berenko stirring up action in the hallway. It would only be a matter of minutes until his attempts at creating panic had succeeded, and he would return to either gloat over or bury what remained of Nick Carter.

This definitely offended my sense of dignity. Escape was called for, and without delay. I picked up Wilhelmina and dropped her into her holster. I staggered to the window, gracelessly I'm sure, but then aesthetics were not my concern at the moment.

The window shot up and I stared at the one-story drop that faced me. There was no choice. I pushed my body out onto the sill and twisted myself around. Using my left arm to the best of its capacity, I dropped to the ground and rolled.

I landed clumsily, but intact.

Berenko's face appeared at the window, just in time to watch me depart through the open court toward my car. There was victory on that face, an expression that filled my mind with rage.

Your time will come, you Commie sonofabitch, I hissed to myself, but I knew I was in no condition at the present moment to do anything about it. Survival came first.

My pace was anything but steady as I struggled to reach the Citröen, but finally I hauled myself behind the wheel and pointed the nose toward the apartment where I had left Robin.

I arrived at my destination slightly more numb, and with only a few near-miss accidents to jeapordize the effort. I found the bell labeled 'Mousif,' and rang it for all it was worth. Robin answered the door, accepting my crumbling body in the process.

She walked me to the stairs, machine-gunning questions as she went. I ignored them, stumbling up the steps, mutely seeking my way toward safety and comfort.

Silence was broken only when I had collapsed onto the soft cushion of the apartment's one bed.

"Your friend," I mumbled. "Is she . . . where's your friend?"

There was a glimmer of humor in Robin's eyes as she answered. "I told her I was traveling with you. She gave me a brief lecture on the basic uselessness of men, and huffed her way out the door. The place is ours until tomorrow. Then she wants us gone."

"Smart girl," I nodded, and then a fresh jolt of pain seared through my arm and turned the room a funny shade of gray. The breath whistled through my teeth as I tried to grit the pain back.

"My God, what the hell has happened to you?" she cried.

"Nothing, my dear. Nothing at all. A mere trifle. A simple game of mumblety-peg that went astray, I fear," I hissed in my best W.C. Fields.

She was obviously not a W.C. Fields fan; but then, I'm not sure I was definitive in my portrayal.

"Take off your coat and shirt," she ordered.

She jumped away from me and ran into what I assumed was the water closet. I obeyed her commands, stripping to the waist as she returned with several strips of gauze, some tape, and a rather strange looking green bottle.

Grasping my arm, she twisted it and held it out over the bare wood floor as she poured the contents of the bottle into my wound. The sensation was not too far removed from the original agony.

"Jesus," I screamed. "What the hell are you doing to me!"

"Killing the infection."

"With what? Saltwater?"

She stared at the bottle for a minute. "It's liquor, I think. It's the only thing I could find with alcohol in it."

I groaned as the pain eased up. "Well, that's smashing, my dear. At least I won't have to worry about infection running through my system . . . it may stagger, but it won't run."

She flickered a grin and dropped to her knees by the bed, working with all the rapt concentration of Florence Nightingale. It wasn't until she was dressing the wound that she again spoke.

"I talked to my people."

"And?"

"An alternative plan has been devised. Like you, they feel commercial travel might be too risky."

I winced slightly as the first winding of tape pinched at the wound.

"Sorry," she said. "They're going to contact one of their people here. That person will rent us a car. It will be dropped near here, the keys left under the front mat for us to pick up."

An uneasy feeling began churning in my stomach.

"We're to take the car and drive to Oran," she continued. "It's about 300 kilometers. There we will locate a Mr. Jouret. He runs a small aviation outfit—hops to Spain and all that. He will fly us to Rabat, Morocco."

"Is he one of your people too?"

She looked at me briefly but didn't answer. The feeling in my gut began spreading.

"Once in Rabat, we're to go to the main airport. My people will have a private Lear at our disposal, which will get us to Capetown. Further instructions will await us there."

She was just finishing up her labors, and I tested out the dressing while I thought through her information.

Once again, something smelled. Lear jets in Rabat, bush pilots in Oran, agents in Algiers. Who the hell was I working for? There are entire nations whose intelligence operations aren't that sophisticated. There were just too many unknowns, and my nerves were beginning to fray.

She started to rise up, and I halted her by grabbing her shoulders.

"Robin, who are your people? Who are you working for?"

She stiffened. ''You're asking questions again. You were told not to do that.'' She tried to move away, but I held her.

''Look,'' I snapped, my temper rising, ''I'm not asking for details. Just give me some answers. If you don't, I'm afraid I may just have to bugger-off home, and let your people clean their own commode.''

Her stare was uncertain but defiant. ''Then, Mr. McDaniel, why don't you just bugger-off!''

I was good for about one more second of rationality. ''Robin, it's not just idle curiosity. I *need* to know. I'm in a high-risk profession; I kill for a living.''

Her body went ice cold. She began squirming to release my grip on her, but I wasn't about to be put off.

''So far I've managed to stay alive by keeping myself one step ahead of the opposition. Anything can happen between here and Capetown. We could get separated, or quite frankly, you could get killed. If that happens, I'll have to have some idea of where to go, or who to contact. The more I know, the better I can operate. In this business, what you *don't* know can kill you!''

Her body was full of tension, but her voice was like a computer printout. ''You'll be given information *when* it is necessary, and you'll be told only what is—''

I exploded. ''I've had enough of that pap! I've almost been killed twice today, and now I want to know why, and for whom! Am I making myself clear?''

My hands were digging into her shoulders, bringing a wince of pain to her face. Her squirming grew desperate, but her manner remained resolute. It was necessary to add further persuasion.

There were two huge bruises, one on each arm, from where the Russian had thrown her against the wall. I grabbed for them, clamping down with all my might.

Her body went stiff, her throat erupting in a scream

as the pain jolted through her body. I released my grip ever so slightly.

"Talk to me!" I growled.

Her head shook back and forth in refusal. I squeezed again, harder. Her mouth shot open and tears spilled from the corners of her widened eyes.

"A group!" she cried. "I work for a group!"

"What group? *Where?*"

"South Africa. The Society. They just refer to themselves as The Society."

We were making progress. I eased up slightly on my hold, but not enough to let her think that pain was very far away.

"I need a little more than that."

She paused a moment, then shook her head slightly, driving off her tears as she gasped to regain her breath.

"You're a bloody bastard, you know that?"

"That's what my Mum tells me. Now, keep talking!"

"I'm working for a group called the Society of Nine."

"Interesting name. Where'd it come from?"

She shrugged. "I don't know really. Nine members, I suppose. I only have contact with one of them."

"And who might that person be?"

"That, Mr. McDaniel, you don't need to know."

I grabbed her again. Her body once more stiffened, but her resolve did not.

"Tear my bloody arms off, if you must, but it's an old friend, and I'll be damned if I'm going to tell you his name!"

I eased up. It seemed pointless to push her too far. "All right, my love. Maybe that's one I don't need. But tell me just a wee bit more about this Society of Nine."

Her body relaxed again. "It's a small group, mostly government officials, who are working independently of their offices to do all they can to see effective black rule in South Africa.''

"Why independently?" I asked.

"You've obviously never been to South Africa, Mr. McDaniel. The white population is not exactly what you would term 'hot' for black rule.''

"I don't need a political science lecture . . . and please, call me Liam.''

For a second she looked as though she might stick out her tongue. "Anyway," she continued, "if they were too open about their desires, they'd probably get their heads liberated from their bodies. Most assuredly, they would lose their positions in government. They feel it is wiser to keep their public faces to the right, but their private actions toward the left. It just so happens that they are also willing to speed the process up a bit in a behind-the-scenes way.''

"Even if it means walking a bit of a legal tightrope?"

She nodded. "They're dedicated men, Mr. Mc . . . Liam. Very dedicated. I only hope that, someday, they can get the open credit they deserve.''

The pride in her eyes and voice was almost touching. "And what's my contribution to this back-chamber revolution?"

She eyed me with distaste. "Your job will be to perform the services you seem to be so good at.''

I lowered my head in a mock bow. "Shall I start squeezing again?"

A flicker of fear passed over her face. "No! Please?" I nodded, and she took a deep breath. "There are some kind of special negotiations going on with the United States. I don't know what they're all about, just that they're happening.''

I gave her my best threatening glare, and flexed my hands.

"That's all I know! I *swear!* They only tell me little

bits of things, just like they'll only tell you bits. Only what they feel I need to know to get the job done, nothing more.''

It made sense. She was an amateur—an instinctive one, and one who was getting tougher by the hour—but an amateur nonetheless. I was sure she was leveling with me.

"What kind of negotiations?" I asked.

"I'm not sure, really. Apparently, America has gotten itself involved in the black rule question, and it's beginning to look like an agreement is possible. I don't know the details, but apparently it involves some rather shaky commitments.''

So far she was right on the money. I decided to prod her along from my own knowledge of things. "And with America in the picture, you can wager ten bob to five that Moscow will be poking their noses about, too. Am I right?"

She nodded.

"Then that would explain it," I sighed.

"Explain what?"

"Why you and I have been spreading our day playing 'Round the Maypole' with the Russians.''

Her mouth slacked open, and her eyes bugged in astonishment. *"Russians?"* she gasped.

For a moment, it was my turn to stare. She honestly didn't know who it was we had been toying with.

"Russians," I nodded. "Just who did you think those chaps in the alley were? The Algerian Better Business Bureau?"

Where there was astonishment before, there now appeared an icy hatred that chilled me to the bone. Her voice was little better than a growl. "Those Slavic sons of bitches.''

"Here, here, is that any way to talk about your White brethren?" I quipped.

''No brothers of mine,'' she spat. ''I hope you take the bastard and blow the brains right out of his Commie ass!''

Bingo! We were getting somewhere. It was time to stop playing the Marquis De Sade, and switch over to Grandpa Walton. I let go of her arms, bringing my hands up to cup her face.

''I take it I'm to remove one of your Marxist citizens out from under whosever fingernail he is residing?''

She nodded. ''I don't know who it is yet, but The Society does. It's someone on the negotiating team. Whatever the deal is that is being arranged with the United States government, this bastard is sharing it all with the Soviet Union.''

Double Bingo! So, someone had located Hawk's leak for him, and I was being brought in to play the plug.

''Liam?''

Her voice brought me back. ''What, love?''

Her eyes were searching mine like a suppliant searching out her God. ''Liam, just for me. Please. Kill the bastard twice!''

I laughed, pecking her lightly on the cheek. ''Impractical, my little muffin. But I promise you, I can make that first one a foretaste of hell.''

A smile crossed her lips and her eyes moistened. Then the emotion passed, leaving something far less definable in its place. I would have to call it perusal, because her eyes refused to leave me.

She was the first to break the silence.

''Why did you kiss me? Back in the alley, I mean?''

There was a shyness in her manner that touched me. For the first time, I noticed she had changed into a sweater and slacks, both slightly too big for her. It only served to make her look that much more vulnerable.

My hands moved off her cheeks, and began toying

with her long hair. "Two reasons, really. You were in a state of near panic, and I had to shock you. What with all you'd been through, slapping seemed like a bad idea, so kissing just sort of jumped up and screamed at me."

She twisted her head a touch, flowing with the feel of my hand in her hair. I continued, my voice growing gentler. "The second reason was kind of selfish."

Her brow wrinkled quizzically. "What do you mean?"

"I just sort of wanted to thank you. What you did in that alley was nothing short of sensational. The slapping was courageous, and saving my life . . . well . . . there are a good many in this world who'd have knighted you if you hadn't."

Her eyes dropped in embarrassment from the praise.

"Besides," I added, "it was impossible not to. You have the cutest breasts this side of the Mediterranean."

A giggle burst from her throat and her face glowed red beneath her dark, rich skin.

Again our eyes held, and again one emotion soon transplanted another. This one was less enigmatic, punctuated only by the slight parting of her full, rich lips.

I'm not the kind of man that needs to be begged.

I returned my hands to her face and brought her up to me, tenderly pressing my own lips onto hers. They were tentative at first, but willing.

I probed gently with my tongue, caressing her teeth and mouth, savoring the sweet warmth I found there. To me, every woman has her own taste. Robin was like a young wine: sweet and bold, whose mere presence in your mouth was enough to intoxicate you.

She slowly began responding, her own tongue returning my affections. I cupped her face tighter, pulling her into me and accepting the sweet warmth of her offering. An eternity must have passed before I finally broke the contact.

"Look, Robin, I'm sorry I had to—"

I never got to finish. Her lips returned, forcefully this time. Her tongue came alive, with a will of its own. Aggressively, she searched my mouth as her breathing began to come in shorter gasps.

At the same time, her hands began to play along my exposed upper torso. Her fingers worked up and down my ribs, her pace growing in intensity, matching the ever-climbing pitch of our joined mouths.

A threshold was quickly reached, a moment when events must either stop, or crash ahead to their certain finality. There was another pause as both of us considered the direction we were taking.

The decision was really hers, and both of us sensed it. It was quick in coming. All the pressures of the day's events seemed to hit her at once. Her body gave a violent shudder, and her lungs collapsed into one giant explosion of air. Her decision was made.

If only for a little while, she needed to escape, to erase from her mind the overwhelming realities she had suddenly encountered. She lunged at me, her tongue digging into my mouth, and her hands, no longer gentle, tearing at my body.

She was a cat, clawing her prey, intent on one more day's worth of survival.

My own desire for release proved no less demanding than her own. My hands went behind her, pulling her into me, crushing her in my embrace. Her lips slid off mine and settled near my ear, her hot breath gasping as she spoke.

"Oh, yes, Liam. Please. *Please!*"

Her lips returned to mine as my hands climbed under her sweater and worked their way toward the soft mounds of her breasts. Her body jerked in pleasure and a burst of air popped from her lungs as I cupped their resilient softness.

Her breasts were firm and full, their nipples taut with excitement. I moved from one to the other, measuring their perfection, twisting at each nipple as her moaning became a symphony of acceptance.

I could feel the pounding of my own passions as my senses began to dull. The pressure in my groin was mounting, almost painful beneath the restriction of my clothing. The movement of my hand across her breasts became an insistent kneading as the rippling shudders of her pleasure pushed me farther into oblivion.

She suddenly broke away from me, her words pouring out between fighting gasps of air. "I need to feel you. Please, let me feel you."

With that she jumped up and tore at her own clothing. I did the same, my own passions surging as each aspect of her perfect body emerged from its cloth covering.

With my own clothing shed, I stretched myself out on the bed and awaited her. In seconds she joined me, pressing herself onto me. I rolled her to my right, and began traveling her body with my mouth.

With each stop of my lips, her hands would dig into my hair, pressing me into her, her moans a joyous accompaniment to the pleasure I was giving her. My roving lips came to rest where my hands had begun, on the full perfection of her breasts. I sucked hungrily at her nipples, alternating between tongue and teeth, torturing both of us into a pitch of erotic frenzy.

At the same time, my left hand slid down her belly, working its way through the down patch of her mound and probing gently at the soft lips of her sex.

She was moist and open, totally ready for whatever I had to give her.

"Yes . . .*yes!*" she panted.

I rolled on top of her, oblivious to any sensation, even the nagging pain in my arm, as I held myself above her. Her hand clutched at me, guiding me into her, her hips greedily rising to accept me.

We both shivered in delight as I entered her, slowly, steadily, not stopping until the hard knob of her pelvic bone pressed against mine.

Rhythmically, I began moving my hips, slowly at first, savoring the deep warmth of her body as it caressed me. Her hands pulled at my lower back, taking me in each thrust, and demanding the fullest extent of my penetration.

I lowered myself down, spreading myself over her. Her nipples felt as though they were burning into my chest. I moved myself with calculated precision, pressing my hips and rocking my upper body at the same time.

I stepped up my pace, measuring her needs by the deteriorating gasps of her breathing and the demanding pressure of her nails as they raked my back. My hips began churning, driving her into the bed, racing against the mounting insanity of my own release.

Control was becoming very difficult. The hungry demands of her body were pulling me in like a whirlpool. Her hips were pounding fiercely, stroking me, enveloping me in a moist sheath of sexual agony.

Her own desires for climax were no less insistent than my own, as the first waves of orgasm were sweeping over her. Her body gave, first one, then another racking jerk. Her hands ceased all movement, her nails digging into my back as the initial surge of her release carried her in a soaring upward spiral.

Then her hips pressed against me, her sex tearing at my organ like a greedy animal as we came together in a feverish climax.

And then peace. A warm, satisfying, gasping peace,

as both Robin and I collapsed.

For at least a minute, the sounds of our breathing were the only realities in the room. And then she stirred, her arms and legs stretching out, soft purrs emanating from her throat.

With the return of sanity, I became aware of the weight of my body on my injured arm. I rolled to the side, sliding out of her, and moving my hand over quickly to stroke her body. She smiled, her flesh undulating in delight as I caressed her.

My hand roamed her luscious form, only stopping when I suddenly discovered something I had overlooked in the midst of our passion. She had a tatoo, located directly over her right hip bone.

I moved myself down slightly, studying it, tracing its outline with my finger. It was an incredible rendering, in brilliant orange and black, of a leopard; in side view, and in midleap. It was only about an inch or two in length, but the detailing was incredibly exact.

"Don't tell me," I chuckled. "You used to belong to a cycle gang, right?"

"What?" She propped herself onto her elbows. "Oh, that. No, just a drunken moment of caprice, I'm afraid. My youth remaining to haunt me!"

"Care to explain?" I asked, resuming my stroking.

"Well, when one is young, one must find something with which to torture one's parents . . . to express that independence that all adolescents crave. In South Africa, white children usually express their rebellion by adopting the attitudes or symbols of the black counterculture. That was my contribution to my father's graying head."

"What does it mean?"

"It's a popular tribal symbol. Leopards were a powerful predatory force in tribal Africa. It was the black African's symbol of power, virility, loyalty, and all that. Most of the black-rule groups used it as their own symbol."

"Well, whatta ya know," I smirked. "I'm in bed with an African hippie!" I kissed her tatoo as punctuation to my jest.

She ran her hand over my head. "Not really. I just did it to stir up Mummy and Daddy. The closest I have ever been to being *really* political, or ever will be. I should think, is what I do now for a living."

I tried to be coy. "And that is?"

For a moment she refused to bite. But then she giggled. "Do you ever stop asking questions?"

I crawled back up beside her. "Never," I smiled.

She grinned back. "I'm a staff member for one of South Africa's biggest black representatives. I handle travel arrangements, bookings, correspondence, whatever gets called for. I'm paid by the government, but I really consider him my boss."

"Who?"

"Joseph Nikumba."

I didn't mean to, but I must have shown my reaction to the name. Once more, the coincidences seemed to be piling up.

"Do you know him?" she asked.

"A bit. Not much, really."

She snuggled up against me, her eyes getting slightly dreamy and far away. "He really is a marvel. If anyone can put South Africa right, he can. He's a social anthropologist, and he's got some brilliant ideas about how to pull the black tribes together. He's studied them, you see. Even spent his summers as a student living among them. He even married a genuine African tribal princess . . . some tribe in Botswanna, I think."

She suddenly popped up. "Would you like to see what he looks like?"

I had already seen, and studied the man from AXE's

files. But Robin was feeling chatty and communica-
tive, and I saw no reason to thwart her. I was hoping she
would begin to make it a habit.

"Please," I said, my manner impish. "Allow me to
gaze upon this black saint of yours."

"Oh, pooh!" she chuckled, slapping at the front of
my hair. She jumped up and ran to her purse. I laid
myself back, enjoying the sight of her naked body as
she fished out a picture and returned it to me.

She bounced onto the bed, thrusting the photo in my
face. "Isn't he beautiful? Doesn't he look kind, and
intelligent?"

I looked at the face. It was indeed kind and intelligent. A round black face, leaning toward pudgy, with
close-cropped, kinky hair flecked with gray. The suit
was tailored and impeccable, the glasses thick-rimmed
and duly professorial.

I was struggling for an answer to her question, a
teasingly irreverent answer, when something caught
my eye.

I shot bolt upright in the bed.

"What is it?" she asked uncertainly.

I couldn't answer. There, in a corner of the picture,
was a face I was all too familiar with. A face I hadn't
really ever expected to see again, and *never* in this kind
of context.

"Who's that?" I demanded, my finger stabbing at
the photo.

Robin studied the object of my query. "Oh, that's
Bosima, the woman I was telling you about. The Botswana tribeswoman, you know, the Princess."

"Nikumba's *wife?*"

"Yes. Why? What's wrong?"

Questions were wasted. My mind was too numbed to
deal with answers. I could only stare at the picture.

What stared back was two images. The one was the

face in the photo; placid, regal, haughty. The other was the living image of the woman as I had just seen her; arrogant, defiant, and cold.

Nikumba's wife and Berenko's date were one in the same.

CHAPTER SIX

The trip from Algiers to Capetown went without a hitch. The drive to Oran almost had a vacation quality to it. Having broken the ice with Robin, she was now freer in discussing herself and her relation to events in South Africa at least as far as she knew them. The entire ride possessed an easy comeraderie, highlighted by occasional stops to view the wide, blue sweep of the Mediterranean.

The flight to Rabat was less dramatic, but for my purposes, more productive. Robin spent most of the flight asleep, finally surrendering to the pressures of her first day in the covert actions business. I, on the other hand, alternated my attentions between keeping her comfortably nestled on my shoulder, and sorting out the events I had just been through.

We had found our leak.

I had entertained at least a fleeting hope that perhaps Nikumba's wife was getting only surface information, and took advantage of Robin's mood to question her on it. The worst was confirmed. The man loved his African Princess with a passion, and trusted her implicitly. "The daughters of Eve strike again."

With the Russians to guide her, she could work Nikumba, and his love for her, fully and effectively. She would just keep feeding him the apples until the whole Garden of Eden withered around his ears.

Telling Nikumba would be useless. No man believes his wife can betray him. The leak would just have to be plugged another way.

My way.

Once Rabat had been reached, I left Robin to handle our connection with the Lear jet, and snuck in a phone call to Hawk. I told him of The Society, their desire to have me eliminate the leak he had been searching for, and my discovery of just who that leak was.

It fit the pieces of his puzzle exactly. His own search had narrowed down to a very few people, all within breathing distance of Nikumba. He agreed with my estimation that accusations would be wasted on Nikumba. Action was called for.

He questioned me further on The Society of Nine itself, but I was unable to offer him anything more than the scraps I had gleaned from Robin. He promised to dig up what he could for me, and we ended our call with the agreement that I would contact him as soon as The Society had filled me in on exactly what my duties were.

Once in Capetown, we were met by one of Robin's people, who drove us to one of the town's more remote areas. The drive itself took us through the entire spectrum of South African society. We passed through built-up areas of high-rise office, a monolithic testament to the White man's culture. Beyond this were the sweeping residential areas, with the only blacks visible carrying brooms or sporting uniforms.

The closer we got to our destination, the more squalor and deterioration we saw. Even Robin grew somber as we slid past dilapidated homes, once the residences of the white elite but now memories of an earlier splendor.

It made a sad contrast to the gardens and lush groves of the residential whites. In areas like this, no matter where in the world they might be, are planted only the seeds of hate and frustration; and the only crop that grows are the rows upon rows of rifles, and knives, and bodies, that are the daily fare of the oppressed.

Our own destination proved to be just such a place. It was a poor area on one of the several hills around Capetown, a village of tin huts, thrown together out of corregated roofing and chewing gum and stuck on the hillside with nothing more than prayers to keep it in place.

Our driver departed, leaving the car and walking away with that kind of familiarity that only comes when one is at home. Robin and I explored our safe house, a single room shack, with mattress on the floor, and little else to break the monotony of poverty that surrounded us.

Water would be retrieved at a communal pump, shared by others in the complex, and when it came time to relieve oneself of that same water, a convenient spot would be chosen among the numerous palms that dotted the hillside.

"Rustic, but quaint," I growled, not trying to hide my sarcasm. It was the first comment that had passed between us since the gardens and groves had turned into slums.

Unfortunately, Robin did not laugh. "This is what we hope to eliminate, Liam. I do hope we're not inconveniencing you too much."

Although we had gotten rather close in the last welve hours, business had a way of making her testy. I felt the urge to blunt that, just a bit.

"Inconvenienced? Not really. I mean, it's not the Belfast Hilton, but then I really wasn't expecting much."

The point wasn't lost on her. "Sorry," she whispered.

Having scored my points, it was time to lighten the mood.

"All the place needs, really, is a christening. Don't you agree?" As I spoke, I pointed to the room's single mattress.

In spite of the ride, and all it meant to her, a smile broke out on Robin's face. "I thought you'd never ask!"

A house is not a home, and a hovel is not a prison when you know it's for a day or two . . . and when you have someone like Robin to help break up the boredom of the scenery.

In no time we were both naked, her lovely body lighting up the surroundings like a mirror-ball at a disco.

It was Christmas in July.

We moved together on the mattress, careful in our exploration of one another. There is something about making love in surroundings like this; there is nothing to distract you, nothing to divert your attention but the absolute perfection of body and talent with which you are being bestowed.

Unlike our last encounter, there was no desperation, no psychological demand for escape and refuge. There was only appreciation: me for Robin's sublime physical presence, and her, for the hard, muscled, controlled accuracy that kept me alive . . . both in and out of bed.

The pace was much slower, much more considered in its forays and explorations. She had accepted me by now, viewing the scars that decorated me not as threats, but objects of my personality, to be kissed, stroked, studied, and tasted.

I returned her efforts, examining her with all the interest and fascination of a scholar perusing an original Shakespeare folio. But, where a scholar will search and dissect with his eyes and mind, I delved into this mystery of flesh with my tongue, my hands, and my desires.

By the time we joined, our passions had reached incredible heights of longing. I entered her once more, slowly, carefully, letting the tempo build as my hips established their rhythm.

Her own response, heightened by the firm urgings of my manipulations, grew in intensity. Her body responded to mine, accepting me completely and rivaling my attempts to hold the inevitable to its last possible moment. Together we moved, an ebb and flow of motion, toward a powerful peak.

And then the internal storm exploded, carrying us both on an incredible tidal wave of bliss. She began bucking with all the fury of a trapped animal, desperate and hungry for the freedom of release.

And I accommodated.

I manipulated her mercilessly, thrusting hips and fingers in matched tempo to her demands. And then my own control left me, seduced by the delighted contractions of her sex. I burst within her, spilling the last remnants of my own sanity into the blazing cauldron of our union.

The mutual expression of our passion resounded through the tiny room, filling it with moans of a more human, and satisfying, atmosphere.

And then, silence, warm, satisfied silence.

We collapsed gratefully onto the mattress that was to be our home for the next day or two. For a short while we lay there, gently furthering our explorations of each other's bodies.

But soon, duty called.

We dressed quickly, with Robin assuming more of that tone that indicated the work side of our relationship was now paramount. She took a map of Capetown out of her purse and spread it over the slat-wood floor, pointing out the various key landmarks and byways I would need to know to find my way around.

With one car at our disposal, I would have to play chauffeur. She needed to contact her people for final instructions, and I would need to retrieve my hardware from its current home in storage. It was decided that I would drop her at her location, collect my bundle of goodies, and kill an hour or two before picking her up.

Our path retraced the shacks-to-shambles-to-sweeping-lawns pattern we had traveled before, ending at one of the towering buildings that had first greeted us.

I dropped Robin off, and followed her instructions to the home of Denholm Shipping and Storage.

I parked the car a block away and moved in on foot, just to be sure the place wasn't being watched. Since our first day in Algiers, we had been successful in losing our Russian escort service, and I wanted to keep it that way.

So far, all they knew was what I looked like. It was unlikely they knew my McDaniel cover, and less likely that they could have traced anything down if they did. The only possibility would be if they had uncovered something on the Shipping procedures through Robin.

It was worth a little caution to keep our names off the Russian Social Register.

My efforts proved unnecessary. The place was as clean as Grandmother's kitchen.

Claiming my bundle was even cleaner. It took all of five short minutes, and I was back at the car, loading my hardware into the trunk. I drove back to the area of Robin's building and parked myself in one of the nearby restaurants. It was agreed that she would meet me there when she was done with her compatriots.

I settled comfortably into both a window booth and a double Scotch and water. I watched the steady parade of peons and potentates, the dynamic and humble that seem to occupy the inner circle of every city in the world. I could just as easily have been looking at New York or Geneva as Capetown.

I was about halfway through my drink, my eyes still sweeping the street, when I saw her. The liquor caught in my throat, and exploded back into the glass. I slammed it down, my arm sweeping hastily across my face to remove the dousing I had given myself.

It was Nikumba's wife.

At first I couldn't believe it. She was dressed differently, a tailored gray suit instead of the native *dashiki*, but she had that same haughty, defiant carriage, and that same cold stare as she searched the street for a cab.

I leaped from the booth, slamming down some bills, and raced for the nearby car. She found her vehicle at the same time I did, and I gunned out into traffic, pulling in behind her cab and keeping her safely within tailing distance.

I wasn't exactly sure what I hoped to gain from shadowing her. She could be going anywhere: the hairdressers or the bridge club. Or she could be paying a visit to Berenko. So far, lady luck had been riding on my side of the street, and I thought I might as well take another shot at courting her favors.

There was no doubt in my mind that Bosima Nikumba was the target I had been hired for, and if I could get her now—quietly and quickly—I could return to the titillating world of Nick Carter, gadabout and general playboy, just that much faster.

We reached the no-man's land of sprawling homes, and I held my breath.

Lady luck was still with me.

The cab kept going, the homes thinning out and giving way to the more dilapidated luxury of the slums. No one in a gray tailored suit is going to go marching into this part of town for a quick rubber of bridge. She had to be out on business, and my guess was that business had much to do with Yuri Berenko.

The cab pulled to a halt. It was a dismal area, a street of run-down row houses. She popped out of the cab and made her way into the third door from the end of the street. I passed them up, noting the address, and parked the car a block away.

On foot, I circled the block, finding a point from which I could check out the scenery. The passersby moved in a normal flow, coming and going, with no faces repeating themselves. The only permanent fixtures were two huddled blacks, both dead to the world, and if the several empty bottles scattered around them were any indication, they would remain that way for quite some time.

No heat, and definitely no Russians. I was the only white on the street; a fact that was getting just a little more attention than I cared to greet.

I moved quickly to the doorway, and entered. I found myself in a narrow hall leading back to a single door. The walls were marked with slogans and symbols, most unfamiliar to me. The only words I could identify were the occasional scribbled names of one or another of the black guerrilla movement leaders.

I moved carefully along the wall, Wilhelmina popping into my hands, keeping one eye on the door and one eye on the entry from the street. Once the door was reached, I steeled myself for what might confront me, and burst through.

She was alone, sitting at a well-worn table and gazing listlessly out the window. I was obviously the first to arrive.

She recognized me immediately, and made a quick move toward what I assumed would be a back exit. I cut her off, grabbing her frail arm and twisting her, spreadeagle, onto the table. I frisked her quickly, finding nothing. She was without beads this time, but the memory of how I had overlooked them pushed me towards extreme caution.

"Up!" I barked, using my best German.

She rose slowly. Once up, I twisted her around, checking her out for jewelry of any kind. All she possessed was one stick pin on the lapel of her suit, and I removed it, tossing it into a far corner for safekeeping.

None too gently, I pushed her back into her chair, taking up a position across from her. I plopped myself onto the table, one foot firmly on the floor in case action was deemed necessary.

"Well, now," I quipped, "funny bumping into you again. And where's your playmate?"

Her silence was deafening. I had almost forgotten how completely chilling those eyes of hers really were.

"What's the matter, Mrs. Nikumba? Lion got your tongue?"

Her answer was in crisp, institutional German. "Shove it up your ass!"

"My, my, *my!* Such talk! Is it any wonder they won't give you the vote?"

It worked. If she had a sore spot, it would be politics. I had to keep her hyped.

"Soon, Anglo!" She was all venom. "We'll get it very soon indeed, and your head on a platter right along with it!"

"Really? Well, you'd better break out the big black cauldrons, love, because I'm tougher than you can handle . . . especially when the water gets boiling. Now, where's Berenko, and what's the connection between the two of you?"

For just an instant her eyes darted off to my right. It was right out of the movies. Now, if the script went to form, I was to turn around while she did something heroic, like stop the buzz saw that was closing in on little Nell's tethered torso.

I leveled my gaze intently on her, but owing something to caution, I tuned my ears and instincts behind me. There was nary a sound nor sensation to disturb my concentration.

"Nice try," I smiled. "A little trite, perhaps. I would have expected something a little more clever from you."

"Pig!" she bellowed. "Imperialist, capitalist *pig!* We'll kill you all! Africa is for the Blacks. Out with imperialist domination! The glorious era of Black Marxist supremeacy is about to begin . . ."

And on, and on, and on. I was hardly prepared for the barrage I had opened up. She sounded like the editor of the Tass news service, and it was all I could do to keep from falling asleep as cliché after Communist cliché tumbled from her mouth. I was getting nowhere fast.

She, on the other hand, was moving precisely in tempo with her own goals. It was far too late by the time I really began to understand the meaning behind her words.

Sleep was just what she was trying to achieve, and she had me. It wasn't until her propagandizing stopped, dead in mid-sentence, and the sudden explosion of new sounds spilled from her mouth, that it really hit me as to what she was doing.

She burst forth in a new language, one I had never heard before; a collection of vocal stops and clicks that sounded more at home in the throats of birds or insects than the woman I was facing.

And the words weren't meant for me.

I moved without thought. I leaped and turned, placing Wilhelmina in the relative position of any attacking chest I would encounter.

That was my first mistake.

Where I had expected to find chest, I was greeted by stomach. Wilhelmina barked, stopping the stomach's owner with typical efficiency, but the damage had been done. Even the sound of the bursting door to my right did little to shake me into action.

One is not meant to meet one's first Watusi native under conditions of stress. There's something about greeting eight feet of powerful manhood that just has to give one pause.

And that little pause was all the time his two eight foot buddies, hurling their way through the door, needed to pin me to the table. Wilhelmina was quickly liberated as I mentally reviewed the folly of all I had done for the last few minutes.

One can rely too much on instincts. No matter how sharp those instincts can become through years of use, one day they're bound to confront a new experience.

Seldom had those intincts been forced to deal with *the native*, straight from the bush, skilled in the arts of the jungle, natives so subtle in their approaches that they can kiss the ears of a rabbit before the animal even senses their presence.

I awaited judgment.

Wilhelmina was gone, and the nimble fingers of one of the giant Watusi's had little trouble in locating Hugo. No amount of tensing kept the knife from departing my arm. My only hope was that there was some kind of Watusi taboo on testicles.

There must have been, because Pierre remained totally intact. I sat up on the table.

For a moment or two, the girl continued in her strange tongue, instructing her Goliaths as to how to tend their human rabbit. And then she turned on me, speaking once more in German.

"You shall remain in good company, my white

friend. And, for the moment, you shall remain alive. I will contact Herr Berenko and see what his wishes are where you are concerned. In the meantime, you might do well to contemplate your own foolish life, and the certainty of your death.''

She turned and gestured toward the two eight-foot frames that guarded me. ''It will be they who give you your ride into afterlife. They are savages, yes? Perhaps we will get out the pot, just as you suggested. I suspect you will not prove as tough as you would like to think.''

With an evil grin to punctuate her pleasure at the thought, she departed, leaving me to the care of my native brothers.

I studied the two specimens, and it suddenly struck me how entirely careless I had been. These were the two drunks who had huddled outside the apartment. In my search for Russians it had not crossed my mind to look for local talent.

My stupidity firmly established, it was now time to go to work on brilliance. An exit was called for.

Both men were huge, but neither had shown any great skills as trained fighters. It was more the shock of seeing them, than any finesse on their part, that had done me in. They were bush brawlers. *Very tall* bush brawlers, true, but surely vulnerable.

They did have Wilhelmina and Hugo. In fact, Hugo was currently the center of attention. The one holding my knife had discovered its spring action, and was rapt in his study of the marvelous toy. The attention of both was almost childlike in their study of twentieth century blade work.

Innocence: another mark in the credit column. Added to that was the fact that I knew I had Pierre, and they didn't.

The credits were adding up.

Carefully, I worked my hands into my pockets, my

right hand paying particular attention to the removable seam in the pocket's lining. As subtlely as I could, I removed the tiny gas bomb from its home in the family jewels, and cupped it carefully in my sweating palm.

My motion was suddenly arrested when the giant bearing Hugo leaped at me, his mouth sputtering in its unique language, his one hand pointing out his fallen comrade, and his other springing Hugo in and out in front of my face. His message needed no translation.

I waited it out. Soon he became satisfied with his own native eloquence, and returned to his buddy. I allowed myself a calming sigh, and began thinking through a course of action.

I contemplated just tossing the sphere, and marked the distance to the door. I had no fear of Pierre taking me out, but I just couldn't gauge the reflexes of the man with the gun. Hugo may have baffled them, but Wilhelmina was sitting in the Watusi's hand like a familiar pipe. I couldn't risk his knowing how to use it, at least not yet.

And then it hit me.

If Hugo had so amazed and occupied them, how would they react to Pierre's round, seamless, plastic perfection? If one of them could become enraptured wth Pierre's shell-like simplicity, perhaps they would ignite it themselves. That could give me the edge I needed.

There was a note of irony in it, too. It had been the skills of their native life that had done me in. Perhaps the marvel of my twentieth century world would nail them. It was the only chance I had.

With a gentle shove, I rolled Pierre onto the floor. The two giants froze as they watched the tiny ball drift to a halt.

The one holding Hugo was the first to react. He burst into laughter and rushed over to grab Pierre. He studied it, turning it over in his fingers, and applying every pressure to solve the riddle it presented. Then the smile was gone from his face and he glowered in frustrated confusion as he turned to me.

My pulse nearly stopped as he raced over to me and shoved the lethal pellet into my face. He was not gentle in his handling of the object. He was gibbering in tones loaded with question marks.

Now it was my turn. I had to gamble.

Moving my hands up slowly, so as not to make anyone nervous, I took Pierre and beckoned the giant to step away from me. Slowly I began tossing Pierre from one hand to the other, waiting for the native to catch on.

He did.

A smile burst across his face and his hands began waving at me to throw him the object. This was my moment. I opted for throwing in the direction of the gun-man, hoping to burst Pierre on the wall next to him, and make my move for the door at the same time.

I threw the ball, hard and fast.

A miscalculation.

It's difficult to gauge the armspan of an eight-foot opponent, and once more I had underestimated the cat-like reflexes of the primitive man. Their lives, all too frequently, depend on movements of suddenness and accuracy.

His native skills were honed on just such games as this.

The giant caught the ball, bubbling over in laughter, as he held his prize up for all to see. Another round of chattering filled the room as he danced in victory.

And then he did a very surprising thing. He turned without warning and fired the ball to his friend with the gun.

This man's reflexes were no less admirable than his own. Before I knew it, the two of them were engaged in a childhood game as old as man himself. I prayed silently that neither would attempt to test my skills, and did what I could to ready myself for my dash to the door.

For several throws, the two seemed stalemated. And then the giant with Hugo paused, studying his opponent. The game of ball may be millenias old, but human nature is even older. Cheating must have begun when the first single cell decided that, by joining with other cells, he could tilt the odds and dine with impunity.

And this eight-foot universe of cells was bound to carry on the tradition. He noted his partner's left hand, duly occupied with Wilhelmina, and therefore useless in the contest. With the speed of realization, he threw Pierre as hard and as far to the other man's left as he could.

The other man tried his best, throwing his right arm around, but to no avail. Pierre passed him and burst into fragments against the wall.

I could not have asked for more.

The bomb erupted into vaporous activity, the gunman's face not two inches from it. On top of that, his valiant attempt at catching had left him with his back to me. I took full advantage of it. I charged for the door, tearing it open, and hurled myself out into the hall.

I turned quickly to see if I was being pursued.

The gun-toter was already slumping to the floor, his buddy frozen in confusion. The man just stood, his bewilderment rooting him in his tracks, and allowing Pierre's deadly vapors to enfold him.

Within seconds, he was joining his fellow tribesman in eternal slumber.

I moved out of the hall and into fresh air. The street was clear of opposition, and I had only to allow a minute or two to let the room clear, and I could retrieve my weaponry.

The minutes refused to hurry, but timing was still on my side. Finally the room was safe, and I liberated my equipment from the clutched hands of the natives. I moved again toward the door, intent on exit, when something caught my eye.

The third native, the one I had shot, was lying on the floor, his shirt torn open from Wilhelmina's blast. He was covered in blood, but from beneath the flow of his injury. I caught a glimpse of shocking orange.

I moved to the man and tore open his shirt. On his belly, just below the bottom rib, was a tattoo, very distinctive, and very well executed. In curiosity, I checked the other two men, and they too wore the symbol in orange and black.

It was a leopard, in side view, and mid-leap, the same tattoo I had discovered on Robin's belly.

Robin's words drifted through my brain. *The leopard is a common symbol, used by many of the freedom groups.*

Well, maybe so, but these tattoos were identical in design and execution . . . as if they wre drawn by the same hand. It was just one more coincidence in a mission that was beginning to drown in coincidences.

My guts were gnawing at me again.

But it would have to wait. I would find out more later, when I saw Robin. The trick now was to get to Robin before help arrived. I grabbed Hugo and Wilhelmina, and made for the car.

No one interfered, and I struggled my way through the unfamiliar streets, aiming myself for the large cluster of high-rises that marked the sky. When I finally found the restaurant I had so hastily deserted, Robin was waiting.

I approached her, intent on apology, when her face shut me off. She looked like a walking apparition of death. Her face was white, no mean feat for a girl with her complexion, and her hands were trembling, curling around a drink of what looked like straight bourbon. Three fingers deep, and not even an ice cube to temper its effect.

I slid quickly into the chair opposite her and leaned forward until my face was only inches from hers. "Start talking."

She took a deep swallow from her glass, gasped a moment, and finally spoke. Her voice quivered even more than her hands. "Your target . . . they've told me who you are to kill."

Suddenly I understood. As close as she was to Nikumba, she was probably just as close with Bosima. "Look, Robin," I said, trying to make my tone as soothing as I could, "I know the target, and I know how rough it must be for you. But it's got to be done. You know that, don't you?"

It was agonizing for her, but the head nodded yes.

"Good. Now I need to know just how, and when, I'm to take her."

An expression of confusion broke through the gloom.

"Her? Her . . . who?"

"Bosim," I answered. "Nikumba's wife."

She looked at me as though she only wished it were Bosima. My own confusion suddenly grew.

"Wait a minute, Robin. The target *is* Nikumba's wife, right?"

Her head shook slowly. "No."

"Then who the hell is it?"

For a moment she didn't answer. Instead she pushed her glass across the table, right in front of me. When she did speak, her voice was even and quiet, like a preacher giving last rites.

"Your target, Liam, is Joseph Nikumba himself."

CHAPTER SEVEN

The next three days passed like a nightmare. From the moment Robin had spoken Nikumba's name, designating him as the target, logic and sanity seemed to take a vacation.

I immediately called Hawk and lowered the boom on him. As I suspected he might, he blew through the roof. I half expected him to climb the phone cables and ring my neck. "Proof!" he had screamed. "Don't make a goddamn move without solid *proof!*"

It was agreed that I would push Robin to the corner if I had to, but I was not to even contemplate moving without solid goods on Nikumba. Hawk said he would throw an emergency team into the field and come up with everything he could on his end.

And push I did.

I'm not always proud of the things I have to do to win the game, but winning is what I'm paid for. I used every detail I had come to learn about Robin to get what I wanted.

I used her affection for me, her affection for Nikumba; frightened her with suggestions that she could be being manipulated to eliminate an innocent Nikumba; screamed Moscow, whined my own fear of the target; and finally, even came within a hair's breadth of dumping my cover, and spilling the whole caper.

But finally, she did give. She agreed to let me meet with her friend in The Society, and let him confirm the horror.

That had been day one.

Day two had passed in an even more surreal landscape, a landscape of photos and tapes, of eyewitness accounts from agents, of reconnaissance reports. All those things that slowly drive the nails into any traitor's coffin.

And in almost every instance, there stood Berenko. No doubt about it, Nikumba stunk. In black and white, and living color. Bosima was no more the leak than I. She was a courier only, a courier for her husband, Joseph Nikumba.

I was saved the unpleasant task of relating this to Hawk. He contacted me first. His own team had learned the truth.

It's funny how difficult it is, sometimes, to uncover information. You learn you've got a mole, and the field has many candidates. Some you don't want to be guilty, some are too important and you pray for their innocence. Then suddenly things narrow down to one or two, and then the seemingly random pattern of lives, or the apparent innocence of desires and comments, start to come together into a completely different picture.

Nikumba was definitely the man with his finger on the shutter, and the picture looked grim.

The moment Hawk spoke to me, I knew in my guts just which way the cards would be falling.

"Nikumba's code name has been updated," he said, his voice showing more fatigue than I had ever known. "He is now to be referred to as *Judas!*"

Hawk went on to explain the ramifications of what this new turn of events would mean. Most of it I had already figured out, but Hawk was in no mood to have his thought patterns interrupted or enlightened. It was as though, by discussing it, he could make it go away.

The upshot of the whole deal was this:

Nikumba was the main key to South-African Black government. He owned the blacks themselves, and by virtue of pulling America into the picture, he now owned the whites. The announcement of his take over, as an interim-ruler until national elections could legitimize his rule, was only one week away.

Had we not discovered his duplicity, events would have gone thusly. He would have assumed leadership, the American interests, already setting up, would have slipped into high gear, and America would begin the delicate process of tying Namibia into the South African macramé.

Welcome to the land of milk and honey.

But, with Nikumba clearly in the Russian camp, a new scenario emerges.

He gains power, and the world rejoices. The United Nations lifts its embargo, and South Africa dives into the world economy, just as intended. American corporate interests set up their facilities and everyone pops champagne, pats each other's back, looking forward to unlimited profit and prosperity.

And then, the crunch.

Suddenly Nikumba switches gears and raises the banner of Namibian independence. He throws his entire administration behind the S.W.A.P.O. cause. And what do the Russians do? They back out gracefully.

"Yes," they say, "we have backed Namibian independence because the U.N. says they are independent, and we do our best to support the decisions of this most noble forum of universal thought. But now, South Africa has seen the error of its ways, and has thrown off the yoke of imperalist domination that has been perverting it."

But, lo and behold, guess what happens next?

Suddenly Namibia ties itself to the Nikumba comet, voting him as their true representative . . . a reality I

was sure the Russians were promoting at that very
moment.

Then what?

Nikumba gracefully accepts this Namibian mandate
(well ahead of the one *we* intended), he accepts the
responsibility of rule (well outside the framework we
had envisioned), and begins lavishing all those benefits
(that we have provided him with) upon the under-
privileged members of Namibian society.

Our industrial complexes are seized, the Russians
are invited in—only in an advisory capacity, of
course—and life begins to take on a new "enlightened" kind of socialism; specifically geared to keep the
whites at home, but the Reds in the driver's seat.

Voila! Instant Russian control of diamonds and gold
. . . while America licks its wounds and tries to create
any, and I mean *any,* excuse for objecting to events.

But this time there is one big hitch. We can't open
our mouths without revealing what it was that we were
going to pull off.

Ergo, silence.

It was a fiasco; a montage of misassumptions and
delusion, guaranteed to cut our balls and force us to
dine on them at the same time.

I tried to offer just a hint of hope. "Maybe we can
still negotiate. Maybe Nikumba is just playing one of us
against the other."

"Use your head, N-3. Think!" Hawk growled.
"Any man with the gift for uniting peoples that
Nikumba has could very well yield to the temptations of
power. And there is no power quite as supreme as that
wielded by the ruler of a Marxist government!"

Hawk was right. There would be no negotiating. The
ultimate solution was all that remained.

I was to make damn sure I got clear of the site after
the job was done. Hawk would contact Harcourt and

convince him to have one of his agents in the South African government handle the investigation.

It would then be conveniently "discovered" that Liam McDaniel was the killer, and he was an English racist. Harcourt would then wait an appropriate amount of time, stage a cornering of McDaniel in England, and produce the already dead McDaniel to wrap the incident up into one neat package.

Case closed. Justice done.

Hawk even had me covered should I get caught in the act. Harcourt's man would be the one handling me, and Harcourt would merely slip McDaniel's body into the country. An escape attempt would then be staged, and the real McDaniel—killed in his escape attempt, of course—would be substituted for me, and I would slip quietly out the back door.

The latter was definitely the riskier option, what with Berenko knowing full well who I was. But there would still be little he could say without blowing his own cover.

"The real problem comes if you're nailed in the attempt," Hawk said, an ironic chuckle in his voice. "Then, I'm afraid, you will just have to be your own body!"

"Thanks for the encouragement."

"It'll give you incentive. Good luck, N-3!"

The first task was to work out the details of the caper with Robin. By now she had grown to accept the reality of Nikumba's treachery. Her love for the man turned, quickly to hate. It was almost with relish that she laid out his full itinerary for the next week, looking for the opportunity that would put him under.

But still there would be moments, usually when I was pouring intently over the maps and location photos, when she would slip into a deep silence.

"Hey," I whispered. "You're supposed to be helping me."

"What?" Her head jolted slightly as her attention was returned to the room. "I'm sorry, Liam. I was dreaming. Sorry."

"Thinking of him?"

She paused a moment before answering. "No, not really. I was thinking of innocence . . . mine, that is, not his. I was thinking of a time, far too long ago, when causes—black or white—meant nothing to me."

It must have been long ago indeed, because it was a very young girl that was romping around behind those eyes. "Was this in Johannesburg?" I asked.

"No. Actually I was raised in Zaire. It was the Congo then, and my father was very active in government, and very committed to the black cause. He would discuss it with me, but I was far too young for causes. I was too busy being a little girl to care."

That little girl was still visible, even now. A deep sigh shook her shoulders before she continued.

"My father's efforts helped to win the Congo its independence in 1960, and that's when it stopped being home for him. He was the kind of man who needed causes; without them, he was lost. So he obtained a position in Johannesburg, and took up the banners once more in South Africa."

"And that's when you joined in his efforts?"

She smiled. "More or less. He was for black rule, but through peaceful channels. As I told you before, I was an adolescent at that point, and fully involved in the dedicated process of aging him to the best of my ability. That was the period of the tattoo, when I embraced only those philosophies that included violence."

"How long did that last?"

Suddenly her face darkened. "Until he was killed."

I felt slightly awkward witnessing the memory. "Sorry," I muttered.

She shook her head, the deep-felt emotion evident on her face. "It was the rebels. They had set up a bombing, in a white restaurant. My father just happened to be sitting there when it went off. He died instantly, they tell me. There's something to be said for that, I suppose."

There was another pause, and another sigh.

"So, suddenly, rebel causes lost their appeal for me. My greatest regret was that my father died thinking that I condoned the very instrument of his death. I'm not sure I'll ever shake that feeling. So, whether from guilt or a genuine attack of common sense, I'll never know, but I jumped into his shoes, doing my best to further the black cause through legitimate channels . . . within the system, if you will."

"And you tied yourself to Nikumba."

"Yes, I did," she nodded slowly. "He became a sort of embodiment of my father, a substitute. I grew to worship him . . . and now . . . now . . ."

She had hit her limit. For the first time since the horrible truth came out, she cried. It was slow at first, a few dribbling tears, but all too quickly her body threw itself in, shattering her frame with racking sobs of agony. Her hand came out to me like a drowning soul.

I broke from the table, holding her, stroking her, trying to still the turmoil within her.

"It was his!" she sobbed. "It was *his fucking symbol!*"

"What?"

"The tattoo!"

I suddenly remembered the three hulking giants I had encountered in Bosima's rendezvous.

"And now," she cried, "if I could, I would cut the damn thing off my body with a knife!"

She collapsed in another wave of pain, and I held her tightly as she fought to regain control. It was several minutes before the well of tears ran dry and the heaving shoulders set themselves straight again. When she finally looked up at me, her eyes were clear and her jaw was set in determination.

"We have work to do, Liam. Let's get to it."

The plan that evolved was simple.

Nikumba was scheduled to speak the next day to a huge gathering of blacks in Windhoek, Namibia. The speech was to be delivered in a park, and Robin displayed a detailed knowledge of the area. Directly across from where Nikumba would address his audience was a three-story building. From the roof of the building, I would have a direct shot on my target.

The next problem was how to get up there, and Robin provided a solution.

The building was well within the range of my rifle, but far enough away from the dais that the number of guards cruising the area would be minimal. At exactly five minutes prior to Nikumba's taking the stand, Robin would come to the front of the building and create whatever excuse necessary to lure away any guards present, using her position as a Nikumba staffer to do so.

I was then to take advantage of the guard's absence to enter the building and make my way up the three flights of stairs to the roof. The rifle was to be strapped to my body, beneath my clothing, with its various attachments tucked neatly into pockets. Once on the roof, I was to assemble the weapon, and take Nikumba the second his speech began.

I added the precaution of a "fall back", in case there should arise some unforeseen occurrence. I told Robin that she was to follow her part of the plan faithfully. She was to wear a red scarf for the event, and when the time came to distract the guard, I would watch her from some point of concealment. If all was as planned, I would know it by her continued possession of the scarf. But if something went wrong, she was to drop the scarf into her purse and appear to the guard without it. Its absence would tell me that I was to abort the mission until new plans could be devised.

The next question became that of escape. Robin again offered the solution. The Society would provide me with a guard's uniform. Once the mission was executed, I was the dump the weaponry into one of the air shafts that opened onto the building's roof. I was then to pull my pistol and roam the building, just as any guard would, supposedly looking for the source of the gunfire.

In the confusion, it was very unlikely that any of the real guards would start checking I.D.'s, so I was merely to work my way back out of the building, where I would be met by Robin, and the two of us would find our way out of the area and back to Cape Town, where I would be paid, thanked, and sent on my merry way.

The plan sounded solid. Unknown to Robin, I would improvise just a bit, leaving the hardware for Harcourt's address to find, and thereby wrapping the whole project with the bogus appearance of the real McDaniel in England.

Other than that, it would be business as planned, with me departing Robin in Cape Town and thumbing my way back to the States on one of our CIA flights.

And so it went. The third day was spent in traveling to Windhoek. The Society provided us with another safe house, little better than the one we had been given in Cape Town. The difference this time was I didn't have Robin to break the boredom.

She was tucked in with the rest of the Nikumba

contingent, in their fancy hotel. I had only my thoughts and one frayed uniform to keep me amused.

On the morning of the caper, I passed the time by checking out my equipment. I oiled and cleaned the rifle, practicing religiously the steps involved in assembly. I donned the uniform, and carefully concealed my arsenal beneath the oversized coat I had been given.

As the time grew near, I cabbed my way to the sight, memorizing a map of the city, just in case it became necessary to find my own way out.

I took up my position across from the building and awaited Robin's appearance.

In the distance I could hear the echoing clamor of one of the speakers. In front of me stood one guard, casually pacing the street, his eyes searching for anyone that might look suspicious.

Robin appeared right on time. The narrow ribbon of her bright red scarf told me all was going as planned. She talked for a moment with the guard, and in seconds the two of them turned the corner, leaving me my opening.

I moved quickly and cautiously across the street, keeping my eyes open for any unexpected company. There was none. Things were moving, once more, with that kind of controlled perfection that always makes me nervous.

I entered the building and swept the vestibule in one glance. Nothing.

I moved to my left, making my way to the wide, flaring staircase leading to the roof. No sooner had my foot hit the first step, than success seemed to crumble around my ears.

The sound as it rumbled from behind me, was very determined, and very commanding. With just a touch of accent. "Carter!"

I halted in place and slowly turned to face the man I

already knew as the source of my name. "Hello, Berenko. Why is it we just keep bumping into each other?"

He was standing about twenty feet away. He had obviously been concealed in one of the several alcoves I could now make out behind him. He was stern faced, and clutching a pistol.

"Carter, I am about to prevent you from making a very serious mistake."

I was mentally measuring distances and odds, stalling him with patter until a move would reveal itself.

"Are you now?" I said. "Well, what did I do to deserve this honor?"

Berenko was no dummy. You don't end up next in line to run the whole Moscow ball game without gaining some smarts along the way. With a quick gesture of his hand, he signaled into one of the nearby alcoves.

Out stepped one of his Slavic brethren, and he was not alone. To my complete surprise, there stood Robin, scarf in tact, and fear written all over her lovely face.

As if in answer to my silent question, the door I had just entered through popped open, and in stepped two people. One was the guard I had just seen removed, and the other was a Robin look-alike; dressed the same, buried in a dark wig, and scarf in place, just as I had seen it on the street.

Score one for the bad guys.

I looked back to the real Robin. The barrel of Berenko's pistol was nestling itself in the dark strands of hair that decorated her temple.

"One move, Carter, and the young lady is no more."

I forced a lopsided grin. "What makes you think I give a damn."

Robin's eyes blinked in surprise, but Berenko took it in stride.

"I've given your files some time, Carter. You are remarkably talented, of this there can be no doubt. But you do seem to have one weakness. You seem to become idiotically involved in some of your contacts, especially the female variety. Careless, don't you think?"

He was bluffing. There was no way he could know whether I cared or not, but I was forced to admit to myself that I had given him his only hope for leverage.

What I was even more reluctant to admit, was that I *did* care. But that was personal, what we were facing now was business. In my own way, I tried to let Robin know this as I dug myself into her eyes.

Bless the sensitivity of the female animal.

She understood. So much so, in fact, that as we all stood, lost in our own individual games, aware simultaneously that Nikumba's voice was registering in the distance, she was the one to break the impasse.

With the first sound of the distant Nikumba, a hard, resigned shroud seemed to pass before Robin's eyes. She became like steel. With only one quick look to me, part "goodbye", part "do something", she suddenly hurled her body into Berenko, sending both him and his leverage sailing back against the wall.

I bolted up the steps.

From behind I could hear Berenko's frenzied voice. "Carter, don't be a fool! Stop him! *Stop him!*"

And then I heard the muffled sputter of silenced shots. I waited for the wall to burst into life around me, but the plaster remained in tact. The shots were obviously meant for another target.

Robin!

The anguish of this thought carried me around the first bend and up toward the second floor. From behind, I could hear the footsteps of at least two pursuers. As I hit the second landing, I veered off to my right, hiding myself around the corner from the stairs.

I ripped off my guard's coat, eliminating one of the obstacles between me and my gun. Quickly, I flicked my wrist, bringing Hugo firmly into my palm.

As the two pursuers neared my position on the landing, I waited until I had judged the lead to be within two steps of me, and then moved.

Bingo.

I leaped out onto the top of the stairs, and the man was just where I expected him to be. I slammed the guard's coat into his face and sank Hugo into his belly. With a push that was anything but tender, I sent him sailing backward into his friend. The two of them toppled backward, the one already a corpse, the other trying to free himself from the obstruction of his comrade's dying body.

A third man was coming into view, and I chose not to give him a target. I moved quickly on up the steps, making my way toward the roof, and Nikumba.

As I climbed, I unstrapped the gun from my midsection, assembling it as best I could under my hurried circumstances. The gun was more than cooperative, snapping into place without problem. From my pocket I dug one of the three exploding shells I had brought along, and the silencer.

These, too, fell into position on the rifle with no difficulty.

From behind, I could still hear the steady pounding of two sets of feet, with more feet distantly following their lead. It was time to buy just a few seconds more.

I hit the third landing and dropped into a crouch. Carefully I spun, keeping my body as low as possible, and training the muzzle of the rifle down the stairs. With three shells in my pocket, one could afford to be wasted.

The two men hit the landing. Neither was giving

even the slightest thought to caution. They were coming full steam.

I pulled the trigger. It had been my intent to take them both. I aimed the rifle at the first man's shoulder, confident that the force of the exploding shell would take him completely out of the picture, and hoping that the bullet would travel through him, nailing the second man at the same time.

But, for once, Fate eluded me.

Man number two proved too quick for my purposes. No sooner had he detected the sudden halt in his friend's movement, than he hit the floor. The first man's shoulder burst into a shower of bone and muscle as the bullet tore through him, but the shell slammed harmlessly into the wall behind him.

The body tumbled on top of the second man, providing me with precious seconds, but not the minutes I had counted on.

I was up and moving before the second goon could regain his equilibrium. I bolted down a narrow hall, to an unmarked door I knew would let me out onto the roof. I tore it open, moved through it, and slammed the door behind me.

I found myself in a tunnel-like stairwell, facing one last flight of steps, and a door that opened onto the roof. I moved my hands frenetically, looking for some kind of latch to impede the progress of the man behind me.

No way. When lady luck turns her back, there's just no getting her to take a second glance. I popped another shell into the rifle, evaluating my odds at the same time.

I would just have to make the roof, leaving the second door open behind me. At this point, I wouldn't even entertain the hope of there being a latch on the second door. I would gamble on the fact that the jerk behind me would see the open door, remember his pal toppling over him on the landing below, and pause; get cold feet just long enough for me to get off one clean shot at Nikumba.

I moved, racing toward the droning sounds of my target as they slithered in through the second door. And then, without warning, those sounds grew incredibly loud.

I looked up and found the second door open, with Bosima defiantly filling the gap. In each hand was an object; beads. Exactly like the one that had impaled my arm in Algiers. I knew that each of them would be graciously dipped with poison, and both intended for me.

I froze.

From behind I could hear the door swing open, and I knew without looking that my assailant was sizing up the width of my back in his sights.

Things suddenly looked very bleak.

The staircase was barely wider than myself. That eliminated action to my left or right. But something had to be done. There was still up and down.

I pinned my eyes on the girl. Her hand stood poised, ready to launch its deadly missile at the first sign of movement from me. I could only assume that the man behind me was doing the same.

That is, if he wasn't already squeezing the trigger.

I moved.

I swung the rifle up, pointing it at Bosima, making very clear my desire to remove her from the face of the earth. But at the same time, I threw my feet out from under me. Hitting the steps was no picnic, but the pain would be more than justified if the results would materialize.

And they did.

At the first sign of action from me, both parties—

Bosima in front, and the man behind—made their moves. Unfortunately for both, I was no longer in the middle. The dart and the bullet passed inches above my prostrate body, both finding homes in their opposite member's bodies.

The guard behind me crashed to the floor, the screams from his throat ample testimony to the potency of Bosima's native poison. Meanwhile, Bosima herself was anything but silent. The bullet entered her smack in the belly, and her own cry echoed its way down the stairwell.

I waited until she had hit the roof until I once more rose to move. I took the last few stairs three at a time, slapping the scope into place as I went. It was this activity that proved so costly.

With my eyes intent on mounting the sight, they had little time to keep Bosima in view. The woman was thoroughly gutted, but quite alive nonetheless. I leaped out onto the roof, and stepped over her body.

I never saw her strike.

Her other hand, still fully occupied by the second dart, jumped into action. The dart found a home in the back of my calf, and sent me stumbling down onto the roof in the process.

I turned the barrel of my gun toward her, but that seemed to be her finale. Having spent the final reserves of her energy, she collapsed into silence.

It was Nikumba's voice that finally brought me back to the task at hand. The pain was already beginning to climb my leg as I stumbled to my feet, prepared to sprint the last fifteen yards to the edge of the roof.

The first step onto my skewered leg told me just how difficult it was going to be. The poison was already streaming into my system, and my efforts to complete my mission would only speed the progress.

C'est la vie. Such is the life . . . and death . . . of spy work.

The mission was all there was left to me. I knew full well that with a leg full of dart there would be no escape: Harcourt could save his efforts. Nick Carter was going to provide his own corpse for the final show. Well, so be it.

The final show was going to be a ballbuster.

I moved toward the eaves, the world beginning to spin through the sudden fog that was gripping my brain.

Push, Carter, push! Ten yards, that's all. PUSH!

I forced myself forward, hefting the rifle into position at the same time. It must have weighed a thousand pounds. The sound of my own breathing was amplified ten-fold, tormenting me even further, threatening to blast out my ear drums.

Five yards. Move! You must keep . . . keep . . . keee . . .

Behind me, the door slammed open and Berenko's voice boomed across the pitch surface.

"Carter, don't! You don't know what you're doing!"

I so wanted to believe him. The coldness that the poison had first introduced into my body was now turning warm, deadly warm, soothing warm. And his voice, so sweet, so content, so friendly, really.

Maybe I could take just a short nap, just . . . sleep. Then I could kill Nikumba . . . then . . . NO! MOVE! MOOOOVE!

I thrust myself forward for the last few feet, raising the leaden gun as I fell.

Too late. Too many Nikumbas!

The park was a kaliedoscope of movement; one large mass of humanity spinning crazily in front of my eyes.

Moving target. Take your time. Aim. The man be-

hind you, the one shouting "Don't shoot" . . . the nice man with the "don't shoot" . . . WON'T shoot . . . won't shoot . . . can't shoot . . . Jesus, I CAN'T SHOOT!

My mind screamed on as blackness enveloped me.

CHAPTER EIGHT

Desperate visions, slices of my life, floated by in random order. I was traveling an eerie landscape peopled by faces from my past, my present, and other faces . . . born of imagination.

The black girl flew in on the back of some composite creature, her dart hanging in front of her like some ancient knight's lance, huge, oversized. I fought, but to no avail. Her dart surged forward impaling itself, once more, into the back of my leg.

But why was the pain registering in my arm?

So this is death. An eternity spent wandering one's own fears and thoughts. A forever movie, built from scraps off the cutting room floor.

Again the lance chased me, again the weapon found its home in the back of my leg, and again the pain registered in my arm.

Somewhere in my brain a voice was screaming, *Follow the pain. The pain is freedom!*

The pain in my arm grew, pulling me out of the frightening darkness of my own psyche and into the light.

My eyes fluttered open, greeted by the hazy, misted halo of a single light. I stared at the source, waiting for focus to return, each second growing more agonizing as the image tightened into the recognizable form of a light bulb.

My head began pounding as the light seemed to carom around in my skull. It was a welcoming kind of agony. There was something about it that smacked of *life*.

And still the pain in my arm.

Once my eyes had cleared, I looked to my right. I was greeted by the sight of a rather pudgy, balded man. He looked almost cherubic, smiling and kind, as he withdrew the needle from my arm.

''Thought for a minute we had lost you,'' he said, his voice thick in its Russian accent. ''But you are still with us, no?''

I wasn't yet convinced. The man stood and collected up his belongings, speaking to me in soft, soothing tones.

''You should rest for a while, Mr. Carter. When you feel strong enough, you are to avail yourself of all that the room offers. There are clothes, a bath, liquor, all you will need to prepare for Mr. Berenko.''

With each item named, his stubby hand would poke out to indicate the general direction. At the mention of Berenko's name, the memory of where I had been and how I had reached this point grew clear in my mind. But any real understanding of where I was, or what I would confront in the future, remained teasingly vague in my fogged condition.

The gnome continued. ''There is a man outside the door who will escort you to your host, whenever you feel ready, Mr. Carter. Comrade Berenko is anxious, indeed, to chat with you. Rest well, my good fellow.''

With this, he departed.

My instincts were to leap out of bed and find Berenko; but my muscles were still in no condition to accept commands. I drifted off, involuntarily, into slumber, a sleep less hounded by the visions that had haunted me.

Later I awoke, far more able to deal with the complaints of my body. I showered leisurely, allowing the hot, steaming water to wash away the aches in my muscles. The closet was populated with an assortment of suits, all to the remarkable credit of European tailoring. I selected a pair of slacks and a blazer, both labeled from Bond's of London. I added to this an Italian silk shirt, delicately patterned in white on white.

My perusal of the mirror showed me I was returned to the world of the living, the only hint of what I had been through being the still chalky coloring of my face.

A trip to the bar and three full fingers of Glenfiddich repaired that problem.

I was now ready to face my host, and my destiny.

The man outside the door escorted me silently and politely to a waiting Berenko. The halls that we traversed were architecturally quite recent, but the furnishings attempted to create an 'old world', almost European, flavor. There were various people darting about, giving me the impression of a government office building; my further guess being, the Russian embassy.

My guide seemed totally devoid of weaponry, and for whatever reason, there seemed to be no security on me whatsoever. I shrugged and continued in the footsteps of my guide. Berenko was obviously convinced I was not going anywhere, and if the man was that certain, who was I to make a liar out of him?

I was ushered to a pair of oak doors and signaled into the room. I entered. Berenko was sitting behind a huge, dark wood desk, his eyes staring out a window behind him, his lips working furiously at the end of a Turkish cigarette.

The room itself was darkly panelled, not unlike Hawk's office, in its combinations of leather, wood and tobacco smells. It was larger, though, with more thought being given to the creature comforts. A bar stood to my left, and to my right the wall was covered by a large sofa.

Berenko stubbed out his cigarette and rose to greet me. He gestured toward the sofa as he spoke. ''Ah, Mr. Carter. Glad to have you still among us. May I get you a

drink? I detect a slight lack of color still, to your
cheeks.''

"Sounds good," I nodded, taking up a position on
the sofa.

Berenko poured. "Well, Mr. Carter. You gave us a
few nasty moments there. You are a difficult man to
stop.''

"Not difficult enough, it would appear."

He laughed slightly. "It would appear, yes. But, you
will thank me for having done so."

He turned from the bar and approached me with two
glasses. I became aware, as he did so, that the disguise
he had been wearing . . . the blond hair and cheap
clothing . . . had been shed to reveal the Berenko I
knew so well . . . salt and pepper gray, and suits as
tailored and immaculate as his position would merit.
The only vestige that remained were the thick glasses,
now obviously a part of the man, not the identity.

He handed me a generously filled glass of clear
liquid.

"Vodka?" I asked.

He sat himself down beside me. "Indeed! The best,
and chilled to just the perfect temperature. Would you
expect less?''

He was right, and I didn't. The vodka warmed my
still reluctant body.

Berenko gave me a moment to recover my coloring,
and then spoke. "There is much to decide, Mr. Carter.
Perhaps we should get on with events. Do you feel
ready?''

I shrugged. "I suppose."

He settled himself into the sofa. "There is no point in
beginning with futile questions. I could inquire as to
your reasons for being in Africa, et cetera, but I'm sure
I would be no more successful in getting replies than
you were when you confronted me in Algiers. So,

allow me to be the one to, I believe you say it, 'break the ice'. Is that not it?''

I nodded my approval.

"Good," he chuckled. "It is belated, I know, but I will now answer your questions so rudely imposed upon me in Algeria." He moved himself onto the front of the sofa and focused his eyes out the window as he spoke.

"About one week ago, a man was accidentally killed in East Germany. He was a freelance assassin of little record, and apparently had been preparing himself for a mission somewhere in Africa. Our East German comrades did what little checking they could manage, and duly passed their information on to the K.G.B.''

Berenko paused to sip his vodka, allowing me to ingest his information. "The information was then compared by us, against our lists of active missions. His presence in Africa matched none of our intended goals, so we checked further. There was nothing to be discovered about the man, and even less about his mission. Eventually the folio found its way to my desk.''

Berenko paused once more to sip at his drink. I was a little baffled as to why he was giving me his back, and not his eyes. It would seem that he should be studying me for reactions, but instead he was allowing me the relative privacy of my own thoughts. I could merely accept it and listen.

"The case immediately interested me, for two reasons. We have known about your country's manipulations in South Africa for quite some time. You may rest assured, Mr. Carter, that appropriate countermeasures are being duly employed. But, more than this, I became very fascinated with the case for another reason. The man, barring a few minor cosmetic differences, was an exact carbon copy of myself.''

The glass shook in my hand. It was at this moment that Berenko chose to shoot his eyes in my direction, and I felt somewhat embarrassed by the fact that his ploy was rewarded with full confession, written in the stunned look I must have been registering.

My attempts to regain control of my facial muscles were greeted only with another chuckle from Berenko.

"Please, Mr. Carter. I do not do this to toy with you. It is very important that we do not waste precious moments in silly games of "hide the emotions". It is best that we are open with each other."

His eyes awaited my response as I finished the last swallow of my vodka. I turned, handing him the glass, and allowed myself a slight smile. "I'm not as convinced yet as you are. Keep pouring, and keep talking."

He shrugged, sighed, and moved off to the bar as he continued his narrative. "So, we talk some more. I'm sure this will all sound familiar to you, but so be it!"

He poured.

"For the obvious reasons of the man's likeness to myself, it was decided that I should assume the victim's mission, and determine its relative worth to the Soviet Union. I followed the man's instructions, leading me to Algiers, and my first meeting with my contact."

He turned to me and smiled. "The details of that meeting are well known to you."

He returned to the sofa, glasses refilled, and continued his perusal of blue sky through the window.

"From her, I learned in slightly greater detail the extent of negotiations being conducted by your illustrious country, Mr. Carter. A bold plan, I might add."

He turned and raised his glass to me in mock salute. I returned the gesture half-heartedly.

"The lady claimed to represent a small group, Marxist in nature, and dedicated to furthering the socialist cause in Africa. It seems the American negotiations in South Africa were dependent upon the reality of one given man . . . Joseph Nikumba . . . 'the imperialist tool of the United States' corporate dragon'.''

I made to reply, but was stopped by a raise of Berenko's hand. "Her words, Mr. Carter, not mine. I have never been a devotee of Marxist sloganism.''

I sighed and settled back once more into the couch.

"In any event, her philosophies could not have concerned me less, but her goals seemed to be playing right into our hands. She wanted Nikumba killed, thereby bringing the American attempts to a withering halt.''

He turned to me and smiled. "Nothing personal, you realize. Just business, Mr. Carter. It did suddenly appear that fate had dropped a lollypop right into our lap.''

"Don't tell me, let me guess," I added. "You kill Nikumba, make your escape to one of your Communist puppet countries, cover yourself with a story about some East German terrorist hired by an African organization to vent his racist frustrations on one of South Africa's black leaders. You then go on to produce the body, and claim the world's gratitude for ridding it of such an anti-social element.''

Berenko's head flew back in full, robust laughter. "Ah, my friend. It is always a pleasure to do business with professionals, even if they do work for the wrong side.'' His glass emptied in another mock toast.

"More?" he asked. I nodded no. He padded once more to the bar to refill his own.

"So why didn't you go through with it?" I asked.

"Actually, my friend, it was you who first alerted me to the possibility that all was not as rosy as it appeared. When you first burst into the room, I merely assumed you were there to put a halt to good fortune. But you mentioned something to me about an episode

. . . rather grisly in its results . . . with some of my men.''

It was my turn to smile and toast. ''Nothing personal, Yuri, just business.''

He returned the gesture with stunning bravado. ''Business, indeed. Of course, my good man. But one little problem. I didn't have any men, and subsequent checking revealed that no men had been sent by Moscow, either.''

I puzzled at the remark. Berenko returned to the sofa. ''Certainly, you can imagine my confusion,'' he said. ''If these men were indeed Russian, and if they were not mine, then who were they?''

''And who were they?'' I asked.

''A mystery, my friend. Still a mystery.''

We both sipped thoughtfully for a moment. Then Berenko plunged on.

''At any rate, I began checking what I could about who it was that was giving us such a rare opportunity for making fools of your government.''

''And?''

He shrugged. ''Nothing! We could determine nothing of either the girl, or her group. I will confess to you, my American antagonist, that the K.G.B. takes great pride in its storehouse of intimate knowledge, and even greater pride in its ability to generate more knowledge. This inability to puncture the secrecy of a small group of Africans has left more than a few of my comrades just a bit rattled.''

The situation was very familiar to me. In my mind, I could still hear Hawk's voice, filled with worry that bordered on awe . . . ''We can't touch 'em, Nick. They're a ghost group. They're ratting our windows, but they don't leave a trace.''

By the time my thoughts returned, I was aware of Berenko's eyes searching me. He smiled slightly and nodded, satisfied at some confirmation he had observed.

"So," he continued, "I played along with my lady friend, doing my best to get her to reveal her group's plans and intentions to me. It is difficult for me to confess, but I was totally unsuccessful in getting anything but a name from her."

A chill wandered up my spine. "And that name is . . . ?"

He took a final swallow at his drink and relieved me of my own empty glass. He smiled at me before departing for the bar. "I believe you can answer that for yourself, Mr. Carter."

The chill became icier. "The Society," I muttered. "The Society of Nine."

There was no joviality in his reponse. "Yes, Mr. Carter. The Society of Nine."

I needed to think. I rose from the sofa and began pacing the office, forcing my mind to concentrate.

Two men are lured into Africa by the deaths of two unknown assassins. Both men are doubles for the corpses whose mission they will assume. Both are given incentive, in different philosophical and ideological terms, but both are given the same result . . . kill Joseph Nikumba.

It just didn't make sense. The question of *why* remained unanswered.

I turned and nearly collided with Berenko. He held out my freshened glass and talked through that half-smile that he seemed to have perpetually glued to his lips.

"I see you are as confused as I, yes?"

I nodded. Berenko took up a pattern of pacing around the office.

"I have run this little puzzle over and over in my mind, Mr. Carter, and I cannot find an answer. We are accustomed, you and I, to thinking in terms that too often become narrow. We see the world as a contest between the super-powers . . . . *them* and *us*, if you will.''

He paused a moment for effect. "It is perhaps going to become necessary to view a third party in this little scheme. And that, Mr. Carter, bothers me.''

I threw him a questioning look.

His eyes grew hard and distant. "It is inconvenient, Mr. Carter. It is untidy. With us, the game is known. There are even rules, to a degree; certainly there is understanding, and decorum. But this Society is an unknown. They seem to have intentions and goals that do not include either of us. Frankly, Mr. Carter . . . that offends me!''

At first I didn't know whether to take him seriously or not. And then some of his intensity, some of the doubt and uncertainty that the Society represented, began to swirl in my gut.

It *was* untidy, like the man said. When amateurs— even talented ones—begin playing in the big leagues, the game starts to get sloppy. And in a game where the ante is warheads and the bidding unlimited, there is just no room for unknowns . . . especially if they have cards up their sleeves.

Berenko's eyes were measuring me.

"You can see now why I needed to speak with you. You can see why any fencing between us is inappropriate. We have a mutual enigma on our hands, Mr. Carter. I think it would behoove us both to ferret it out, you agree?''

I agreed. I filled Berenko in on my side of the story, watching as the similarity of events and circumstances brought even more worry to his brow. When I had finished, he eased himself back onto the sofa to ingest my comments. I remained pacing.

"So, my friend. It would seem, by events, that our presence . . . yours and mine, specifically . . . were required for reasons not yet known to us. By the way, I have never met Nikumba."

He rose and crossed to his desk, withdrawing a pile of photographs from the top drawer. He tossed them in front of me, watching as the horror grew in my expression.

"My God!"

Before me were a stack of pictures, all of me and Nikumba, all taken as though they were the result of intense reconnaissance and espionage efforts.

"Yes, my friend. It is *us* they want. The photographs are not too difficult to explain. These are probably the same two men who later became convenient corpses to lure us in. It is the *why* of it that we are going to have to take pains to establish."

"Were you able to get any information out of the girl?"

His expression darkened, and he beckoned me to follow him. We moved out through the double doors, and down the hall to a much smaller room. It was obviously designed for de-briefing sessions, with only a single table and two chairs in its center. In one of the chairs sat Bosima, her body slumped in a pose that clearly indicated death.

Berenko spoke first. "She was a very strong lady, Mr. Carter. Very well trained, very willful, and extremely dedicated."

I grew slightly ill as I thought of Robin, her own body no doubt decorating some other room in the complex. "Your methods, Berenko, are like a painter's signature."

Berenko glared, his voice chilling as he answered me. "Please spare me your petty morality, Mr. Carter. I have seen too many of my own agents in just such a condition, to listen to speeches of chivalry and fair play. We are in a nasty business, a survival business, where fairness means extinction. After all, if primitive man had played fair with the animals, we would have gone the way of the dinosaur.''

His point was well taken. "*Touché*," I muttered.

Some of the chill left his voice as he moved toward Bosima's inert form. "At any rate, her death was at her own hand, not ours. Her jewelry, as I'm sure you well remember, was anything but harmless. We were careless, overlooking the lethal capacities of a simple earring. I apologize to you for the oversight.''

To Berenko's surprise, I suddenly moved over to her and tore open her blouse.

"Mr. Carter, please! I'm aware of your reputation with the ladies, but isn't this just a bit ghoulish?''

"Don't be ridiculous,'' I hissed. "Look here.''

Berenko approached as I pointed out to him the tattoo that emblazoned the lower end of her ribcage.

"It is significant?'' he asked.

"I'm not sure. But it does seem to pop up every time the Society does. Robin had one, and the Watusi soldiers that accompanied Bosima also sported them.''

I looked at Berenko, slightly surprised at the gleam in his eye. He stared at me a moment, and then studied the tattoo on Bosima, noting its position on her body. "My,'' he chuckled, "you do manage the most intimate knowledge of your contacts!''

Before I could dismiss the comment, he moved off, leading both of us back down the hall to his office. The conversation continued as we walked.

"Did she tell you anything?'' I asked.

"Nothing she hadn't already said a thousand times. Our methods are quite persuasive. I feel that if she was truly hiding something, we would have found it out. Instead, she seems only to have been given so much information to begin with. I would also be willing to wager, Mr. Carter, that she was recruited because of her beliefs, and these beliefs were then manipulated by the Society for its own purposes.''

We re-entered the office, and Berenko softly closed the doors behind us.

''It is my theory that both the young ladies were hired for their sincere convictions, fed only as much information as they needed to perform their duties. And the nature of that information was always couched in terms guaranteed to appeal to them, and to us. What concerns us is not their testimony, Mr. Carter, it is the testimony of the people who run them. That is what we must learn, and learn quickly!''

Robin's image again floated through my head. ''A little late for testimony from either, I'd say.''

He studied the expression on my face with confusion. ''Forgive me, my friend, but we seem to have a misunderstanding here. You appear to be laboring under the delusion that your girl Robin is dead. She is not, I assure you. She is very much alive, and quite the focus of what it is I suggest we do from this point.''

''But I heard the shot. . . .''

''My dear fellow, it was my desire to catch you, not kill you. The Walthers were merely for emphasis. The only shots fired by my men were with tranquilizer guns. Your lady is quite safe, here in the building.''

The relief on my face must have been obvious.

''Mr. Carter,'' Berenko's tone was chiding, ''you really do allow yourself to get too close to your work. It will cost you dearly one day, mark my words!''

I ignored the comment. ''What is the plan?''

Berenko moved around his desk and stared out the window. ''The best plan would seem to be this. I will return you to your clothes, and place you in the cell with your lady. You will inform her that you have been interrogated, and yielded up no information. You will then tell her you have found a way to escape, which my men will conveniently allow you to do. Do you think you can get her to lead you to her people?"

I nodded. "I think it's possible. The attack by whomever was playing Russian in Algiers, left her quite shaken. I'll simply convince her that you'll have the entire legions of S.W.A.P.O. beating the bushes for us, and our only hope will be for her people to come to the rescue."

"Excellent!" He turned to face me. "I don't suppose she'll lead us very far, but if her contact is one rung up, and then that person takes us another rung . . . eventually we will climb the ladder, you agree?"

"At the moment, it's all we can do."

Berenko nodded, and then led me toward the door. "Please discuss your escape plans with her in great detail, Mr. Carter. The room is thoroughly bugged, and it will enable me to station my men to your best advantage."

"Don't worry, I will."

He paused at the door, flashing me his most winning smile. "And do try to control your enthusiasm. The room is also thoroughly rigged with cameras. I wouldn't want the men watching to become too enamored of the sexual mores of the decadent West."

I returned his smile with more than a little sarcasm. "I dunno, I might just rape her right there on the floor. Could be an incredible blow for freedom, don't you think?"

Berenko chuckled. "Then we'll tape it! I promise you a private viewing at the Kremlin!"

I stepped out into the hall. I don't know how he knew, but my escort was standing right next to the door, ready to take me back to my room, and then on to Robin's cell.

Our progress was only halted by one more comment from Berenko. The laughter had departed from his voice as he spoke.

"One more thing, Mr. Carter. The tattoo. I'm not sure what it means either, but it does add some impact to Bosima's final remark. Even as her own poison was tearing her apart, she found the will to threaten us. It was humbling to witness."

I waited as Berenko seemed to be studying the floor in front of his shoes. His voice was barely above a whisper as he quoted the lady's dying words.

"The leopard shall devour you all!"

CHAPTER NINE

It was with great reluctance that I returned the clothing to Berenko's suite and once more donned the armor of Liam McDaniel. Berenko joined me, and the two of us worked over an outline of procedures for my supposed escape.

Berenko ordered a car to be positioned at our exit point from the building. The car was to be bugged with electronic senders, that would keep Berenko and his men safely behind us. It was up to me to get Robin to agree to take me to her leader.

With all in readiness, I was returned to the cell.

Robin's reaction to my entry was a bit more than I had expected. For one moment she stared at me, uncertain as to whether she was seeing a ghost. Having finally accepted the proof of her senses, she leaped into my arms, tears streaming down her cheeks.

I cannot deny that my own feelings were a bit more pronounced than I would have imagined. For a few brief minutes, as our mouths engaged in a deep, thrusting kiss, all awareness of the hidden cameras seemed to disappear from my fogging brain.

But slowly, reality and the demanding call of duty won out. I explained, not without embellishment, my treatment at the hands of Berenko. I elaborated on the one hand for Robin's benefit, hoping to raise her fears and exaggerate the danger we were in.

"It is imperative that I return with you to your group!"

On the other hand, there was no small amount of joy

in knowing that my descriptions of the man and his evil methods were flowing directly to Berenko himself. I took pleasure in trying to imagine his face as each slanderous appraisal echoed through the room.

The hard sell was working. I could see the fear mounting in Robin's eyes as I stressed the treatment she could look forward to at the hands of our Russian hosts. I let the stick batter her unmercifully before dropping in the carrot.

"Look, Robin," I whispered, "I think I've spotted a way out of here, but there's no point in trying it if we've no place to hole up. Is there any place in Windhoek where we could wait for help?"

She nodded enthusiastically. "Liam, yes! It's a house . . . it's used by the Society for meetings, or briefings, or whatever they decide they need it for. I've only been there once, but I'm pretty sure I could locate it. The only problem is, I don't know if it's empty, and I don't have a key."

"A key is never a problem, love," I chuckled.

So far, I liked the sound of things. If the place was occupied, it just could be by one of the higher echelon. That would save Berenko and me one step on our climb up the ladder. If it was empty, I would just have to put some more pressure on Robin to take me back with her.

I was sure that I could count on Berenko to provide a near-miss or two to keep Robin on edge. She was an amateur; she could be pushed into making big mistakes.

"Look, Robin. This little episode we tried to pull off today is big business. One of your people *must* be stationed nearby to keep tabs. Would they be at this house, or are there other places? We need help, and we need it quick!"

I was beginning to wonder if I was doing too good a

job of rattling her cage. "I don't know, Liam. I suppose there may be, but I just don't know! This is the only one I've ever been to!"

It was time to calm her a bit, or she'd blow it when it came time for action in the bogus escape.

"I'm sorry, love," I said, as soothingly as possible. "I didn't mean to hammer you. The house is fine . . . we'll make contact from there, and your people can alert any locals that may be on tap."

She smiled weakly as I stroked my hand through her hair. We kissed again, this time with less frenzy, and much more of the exploring gentleness we had come to share on calmer occasions. I ignored the cameras, allowing our bodies to merge, and our hands to search each other out.

It was Carter at his best . . . it deserved to be immortalized on tape.

When we finally came up for air, I used the break to begin my explanations of how we were to make our escape. Robin listened intently, agreeing without the slightest hint of fear to each duty she would be called upon to perform.

It was not a particularly brilliant plan, but I was counting on her lack of experience in such affairs to keep her from seeing the obvious flaws. I didn't need an inspired scenario, just a few good acting jobs on the part of the guards for Robin to buy it.

With all in readiness, we took our positions.

Two guards entered the cell with a food tray. Robin threw herself into a panic, as I writhed on the cot.

"My God! He's poisoned himself!" she screamed.

Guard number one took on an expression of appropriate panic, and raced to me. Guard number two held the good tray and drifted over to see what was going on. At the correct moment, a chop to number one's neck put him to the floor. While number two dropped the tray and searched for his pistol, Robin piled into his back, sending him head first into another stinging blow from the side of my hand.

Voila! Two sleeping beauties, care of Moscow Productions.

I relieved the second guard of his Walther. With Robin behind me, we padded our way down the hallway to a carefully concealed rear entrance. Only one more guard, prowling in front of the door, stood in our way. Robin again threw her tantrum, and as she dragged him back toward his buddies . . . screaming, this time, of how I had escaped . . . the butt end of the Walther found a home in his skull.

He quietly fell and kissed the floor.

Within seconds, Robin and I were out the door. There sat Berenko's car, just as ordered. I hot-wired it with ease, slammed it into gear and shot toward the compound gate. As planned, an embassy limousine was conveniently making its way out.

The only deviation to all Berenko and I had discussed was the slight roar of metal on metal as I fish-tailed the car into the left front fender of the limousine. I just couldn't resist the temptation to put at least one small bruise in the Moscow Intelligence budget.

Once clear of the gate, we sailed into Windhoek, Robin shouting directions as she tried to steer us toward the "safe house".

It took just a bit of "hunt and peck", but before long she pinned it down. That we found it at all was tribute to her phenomenal instincts. It was relatively removed from the city itself; a single story, wood structure, that looked as though it may once have been some kind of farm house.

We stashed the car in back, and tried the door. The place was deserted. It took me only a few seconds to work through the single lock that secured it.

Once inside, we looked around. There were four rooms, all furnished meagerly but comfortably. The dust and smell of stale odors told us that it had not been occupied for quite some time. I spotted the phone, and lifted it.

We were in business. It worked.

"Call them, Robin. Tell your friends that they've got two, very shaky birds, in a very flimsy nest, and a whole shit-load of cats just waiting for dinner."

To my dismay, she held off. There was great indecision in those huge eyes. "Liam, I . . . I can't take you with me. I'm supposed to go back alone."

I caught the slight lump in her throat as she said it. I sweetened my voice, going to work on that lump.

"I'll never make it alone, love. I won't last fifteen minutes out there before they come down on me like elephants on a termite."

The lump became a quiver as her uncertainty and emotions raged within her. "A safe place," she croaked. "I can get you to somewhere where you can get back safely. No farther, Liam. I can't. They won't let me."

I felt guilty over my next move. I had to work on those feelings. Maybe Berenko was right. I get too caught up in some of the people I work with. But, in the final analysis, the game must be won.

And to win, you use every weapon in the arsenal.

I reached out and stroked her cheek. My eyes were broadcasting every bit of emotion I could muster, while my mouth talked business.

"Robin . . . what if I said I don't want to go back?"

She looked at me quizzically, but I let my eyes give a silent answer to her question.

Her voice crept through in barely a whisper. "You would stay with me?"

I nodded.

And now she was totally off balance. Her orders were explicit. Do the job, and dump the cargo. But now, suddenly, she'd found herself getting hooked on the cargo. Orders are fine, until they begin getting in the way of one's happiness.

I kept up my prompting. "Robin, this group of yours . . . they need soldiers, don't they? They have people working for them, right? Like the ones that helped us escape from Algiers? I can work for them. I can help them, and be with you. Take me back with you!"

She was crumbling, I could see it. Only the smallest resistance was remaining. All she needed was for Daddy to make it all seem right.

She was practically whimpering her uncertainty. "No . . . I . . . *how?* They won't let me! How will I . . ."

"Listen to me," I whispered, kissing her lightly on the lips. "Don't say anything. Just tell them where you are, and that you desperately need help. Someone will show. They will not, in all probability, have any idea of what you can or cannot do. You can convince them to take us both, and if you can't . . . I can!"

She wavered a moment longer. Her emotions were clearly driving out her duties.

"Just call," I said softly, and planted one more, full-throated kiss on her tender lips.

She moved to the phone, her only remnant of duty being the expressed desire that I not listen in. I agreed and moved into the bedroom. I could hear her beginning her connections as I moved to the huge double window that occupied the bedroom wall.

I looked out down the road and felt a surge of excitement as I saw Berenko's car, a mere speck in the distance, halt. He was, no doubt, narrowing his radio signals down to this house. I watched as two figures departed the auto, making their way, under cover, to surveillance points behind the house. Then I saw the car pull off the road and disappear behind a thick clump of trees.

Satisfied that the back door was duly covered, I stretched myself out on the bed and waited on word from Robin.

Before too long, I heard the phone hit its cradle, and Robin appeared in the doorway. ''They're coming. It'll take about five hours.''

Quietly, she moved over and sat on the edge of the bed. Her emotions still seemed torn within her. As if to assure herself that she was doing the right thing, she began tracing patterns up my thigh with her finger.

''Five hours is a long time,'' I said.

She studied me a moment, and then climbed onto the bed. She nestled herself in beside me, her breast pressing softly into my ribs.

''Do you really want to be with me, Liam?''

I didn't answer. Instead, I turned myself toward her and kissed her. It was a deep, lingering kiss, meant to reassure her. But reassurance soon gave way to emotions of another kind.

Her responses to me grew more and more intense as the certainty of my intentions grew in her mind. Her body pressed hard against me, and I began moving my hands over her, smoothing away the final ruffles of doubt.

With five hours to wait, and no cameras to worry about, there was no reason to halt the proceedings. My lips drifted down, caressing her neck, while my hands popped open the buttons on her blouse. The murmuring in her voice and the firm arching of her body told me that she, too, felt the time could be well spent.

''Take me, Liam . . . take me . . . *now!*''

And I covered her body with mine.

Her breasts revealed, I smothered them with my mouth, plucking at the hard points of her nipples with my teeth. With each nip she would shiver, a gasp punctuating the narrow confines of the room. Her hands nested in my hair, guiding me from nipple to nipple, holding me just long enough to satisfy the mounting demands of her desires.

While my lips worked her upper body, my hands played the lower. I caressed her belly, working my fingers gradually beneath the band of her skirt. I worked slowly and purposefully toward the soft mound of hair concealed beneath her panties. The closer I got, the more her hips would rise to signal their acceptance.

I taunted her, circling her lower belly, teasing her thighs, holding off the final moment of contact. With each near-touch, she would squeal, begging me in sound and gesture to complete the inevitable.

If my taunting was driving her mad, it was doing about the same for me. I could feel the hardness in my groin straining against my clothing. The sweet scent of her passion, and the velvety caress of her skin was pushing me to the very brink of my own tolerance.

And then I touched her, driving my hand against her, capturing her sex in a move that was both gentle and demanding. Her body jerked and then straightened as she pressed herself into me, savoring my touch.

For minutes I stroked her, prodding the escalation of passions that was consuming both of us.

"Yes, Liam . . . yes. Oh, God, YES!" she moaned.

We had clearly reached the point where clothing was becoming an obstruction. Our passions demanded the freedom of flesh against flesh. We both quickly rose and shed ourselves of the hindrance.

Already halfway there, it was Robin who returned to

the bed first. She watched me complete my efforts, her voice purring, her eyes half-lidded, the mere sight of me seeming to fill her with quiet joy.

I finished and started for the bed, but she stopped me. She held me in front of her, her fingers perusing my chest and belly. And where fingers had been, lips soon followed, her tongue tracing lazy, hot patterns.

She worked her way down in the same teasing determination that I had worked on her. Her hands held my hips as her lips and tongue found their way closer and closer to my aching manhood. Like me, she circled and brushed, holding me in an erotic limbo.

And then contact.

Her lips circled me, drawing me in deeply and gently. With complete control, she began working me, timing each advance and retreat of her head with the rolling rhythms of my hips. Her mouth was enveloping me, driving me, whipping the frenzy of my desires into total chaos.

But I refused to lose it, right then.

When I had taken as much as tolerance could bear, I pushed her back. With a smile that bordered on evil, she gave my organ a final caress and then laid herself back, ready to receive me.

I mounted her, swiftly and forcefully, entering her in one firm stroke. We held that way for a second, our bodies pressed tightly together, and our tongues dueling fiercely.

And then I began stroking, in slow, rolling tempo. She joined me, her own rhythms matching mine. My thrusts were deep and constant, while her inner muscles seemed to tear at me, each individual one working independent of the others to drag me into oblivion.

As the pace of our dance built, it seemed as though we were playing a game. Neither one of us would allow the other the glorious release. We were battering each other's psyches, demanding that the other find pleasure first. Our bodies twisted and fought, every trick, every nuance being employed to make the other lose control.

For what seemed like endless hours, the contest continued.

It was not the kind of confrontation that could long remain unresolved. It was one of the few times in my life when I've been out-classed. The drag and pull of her burning sex was taking too great a toll on my body. Try as I might, I could not stop the torrent of my release from bursting through me.

I guess I lost . . . if you can call the scalding explosion of nerves that I experienced, losing.

I burst within her, my body catapulting me into fierce contortions of ecstasy. Assured of her victory over me, she let her own emotions go. She too disintegrated, her body jerking and gasping out the rewards of its efforts.

Gradually, a calm, human kind of naturalness returned. Slowly we settled into one another, savoring the delights of what we had shared.

For a long time we just laid together, ignoring time and place, lost in a small universe that knew of nothing but the two of us. And then we made love again, again testing each other, holding off the glory of climax until the other had crumbled.

This time, victory was mine.

Four hours had passed, four hours of blessed non-existence, before we finally rose from the bed and dressed ourselves in preparation for escape.

While Robin found her way into the bathroom to make herself decent, I tried getting my brain back into high gear for the business at hand. I sauntered over to the window, and stared out. Darkness had fallen, and all I could make out of the landscape was the blackened silhouettes of the nearby trees.

I carefully lit a cigarette, allowing the match to glow

for a longer time than necessary. I was rewarded by a return flare, about a hundred yards off, also held for more time than was required.

Berenko was quite in place.

I chuckled, wondering what Berenko's opinion of the previous four hours' events would have been. He had already expressed his disapproval of my "technique", as he called it, and I could just imagine his face glaring at me in patient disgust.

"And what would you have done for four hours," I whispered to the darkness.

Once more a view of Russia flashed itself on my mental moviola. As always, the picture was gray, and dark. No sun . . . no light . . . no life.

My thoughts were interrupted by the feel of Robin's arms encircling me.

"Liam," she sighed. "It was wonderful."

I grunted my agreement.

And then a note of doubt entered her voice. "But, can it be wonderful forever?"

I turned and faced her. In the glow of the room's single lamp I found it hard to decipher the emotions playing across her face.

"Can it?" she insisted.

I hesitated for a moment. There was guilt about the lies I would need to tell. I've dealt with lying all my life. I've frequently felt remorse for the people I had to manipulate in order to win, but never guilt.

Suddenly I felt guilty. Suddenly I wasn't sure I could speak the lie and keep it off my face. *Yes*, is just too small a word to trip over.

When you can't lie . . . philosophize. Philosophy possesses the unique capacity of obscuring the truth.

"Forever is one of life's monumental words, love," I said. "Everyone always asks it, and no one can ever

answer it. It can't be answered, because it's not a
question. It's an event . . . a happening . . . a judgment passed only from hindsight." I lightly brushed at
her hair. "Let's take it a day at a time, okay? Let's
shoot for it, but let's not try to bronze it and hang it on
the wall."

Any further discussion was halted by the sound of
knocking. With a quick peck on the lips, Robin broke
from me and moved to answer the door. I quickly
slipped into the remainder of my clothes, then joined
her in the main room.

It began to look like trouble from the second I
stepped in.

Robin was engaged in conversation, in a language I
was unable to identify, with three black gents. All three
wore battle fatigues, and sported Kalishnikov rifles.
The conversation was obviously revolving around me,
and the looks on the faces of our rescuers was anything
but chummy.

Finally a resolution seemed to be reached, and one of
the soldiers threw open the door. Robin moved toward
it, and I stepped in line behind her. No sooner had I
reached the first uniform than it became evident that I
was not going anywhere.

The soldier was a good foot shorter than I, but the
impact of his rifle butt more than made up for the
difference. He slammed into my belly, missing my
groin by only inches.

I doubled over, my lungs doing their best to regain
oxygen. Before I could recover sufficiently to respond,
I was dragged backward and dumped into one of the
room's several chairs. The soldier held his arm back,
readying the rifle butt for a clean shot at my skull, when
Robin's voice suddenly filled the room.

The command was, again, in African. Although its

meaning was lost to me, I was grateful for its results. The soldier ceased his actions and backed off slightly, leaving my face and body intact.

I stared at Robin, looking for some hint of my destiny. There was an incredible sadness in her eyes, that told me I had misjudged both her feelings for me and her dedication to duty.

And then she moved toward me, her body and expression reeking with finality. She reached me and bent down, kissing me lightly on the cheek. As she did so, I could feel her trying to plant something into my hand. I took the object and concealed it in my palm.

She then rose up and stared at me. I returned her look, my eyes imploring her as I spoke.

"I take it you're going back alone?"

She nodded. "I must."

"And what happens to me?"

There was no answer. I could see the pain in her clearly, but duty was going to have its way, no matter what. Quickly she turned and disappeared through the door. Just as quickly, one of the soldiers closed it behind her.

For a brief moment, the three men talked among themselves, giving me an opportunity to examine the item Robin had so carefully placed into my hand. It was a piece of jewelry; a long, delicate pin, with its sharp end capped.

Since Bosima and Robin were working for the same outfit, I could guess the lethal potential that the tip of that pin held. Carefully I worked the cap off, and positioned the pin in my hand.

Two things were running through my brain. One: how to get close enough to use my meager weapon, without getting my head blown off, and two: where the hell was Berenko!

Problem one found its own solution. The discussion

among the fatigues was apparently about who was to do the honors. A decision being reached, one of the soldiers passed over his rifle and withdrew a rather ornate, and deadly, knife from his belt. There was a ritual feeling to both the bone-handled weapon and the man himself as he moved slowly toward me.

The man spoke at me in his foreign tongue. It was almost chanting. I allowed my face to register a look of fear, but I readied my right hand, with its pin, for action.

Where the hell was Berenko!

My concerns for anything but survival ceased the moment the blade leveled at my throat. There was no longer any time to worry about Berenko, or rifles. I could only move and hope.

Instantly I lunged, placing my needle beneath the man's sternum and driving it toward his heart. I refused to gamble that the pin might not be poisoned. I went for the instant kill.

The man gave one violent jerk, and then toppled.

As he fell over, the other two came into view, both moving to shoulder their rifles. Every muscle in my body tensed as I prepared to rush them.

I never got the chance. Before I could hurl myself, the windows to my right suddenly exploded inward. The two men danced like puppets as a hail of bullets cut them to ribbons.

The two dropped to the floor and I let out a long sigh of relief. Seconds later, Berenko entered through the front door, his manner as casual as a Sunday caller. With danger removed, my temper found the freedom to show itself.

"What the hell were you waiting for?" I roared.

Berenko shrugged, his nonchalance only goading me further. "My apologies, Mr. Carter. But I wanted to study your technique. Most who see you first hand are quite incapable of telling about it after.''

"Jesus!" I hissed, trying to quell my anger. "For a second I was beginning to wonder if you'd changed your mind about teaming up.''

Berenko's expression took on a sudden note of seriousness. "You have long been a thorn in our collective ass, Mr. Carter. I must confess, there was an instant there when I contemplated ridding myself of your presence. But, the mission at hand proved of greater consequence. So, the thorn continues.''

"Is that going to happen again?''

Again the big man shrugged. "Only prophets, and Russian premiers, can see the future." And then, abruptly, he erupted in a hearty laugh. "Please, my friend, do not take me too seriously. Come. My men are in pursuit of your lady friend. We must join them!''

With that, he turned and marched outside. I sat only a moment more to collect myself, and then joined Berenko in his car.

Robin had apparently departed in the car we had stolen from the embassy, so we were easily able to trail her. The electronic bug in the car led us for several miles, finally coming to a stop at a private airport. Berenko brought his car to rest in front of an open gate in the chain link fence surrounding the field.

Out on the tarmac, I could see Robin and two blacks being held at gunpoint by Berenko's stalwarts. I moved out across the runway while Berenko followed.

The moment Robin saw me, her eyes seemed to light up. The sense of relief she displayed was just too instantaneous and too organic to be an acting job. I was a mere few feet from reaching her, when she burst from the group and threw herself into my arms.

I held her briefly, then broke the embrace.

She stared up at me, pain beginning to replace the relief on her face. "I had no choice," she choked.

"They had their orders. I tried to talk them out of it, but they wouldn't listen. I did what I could for you, Liam. I really tried."

I stared a moment before answering. "I suppose you did. At least you gave me a chance. Thanks."

Berenko caught my eye. His look was disapproving. It was obvious he felt that emotion had no place in the spy trade. Robin followed my gaze, recognizing Berenko for the first time.

"Oh, God, Liam. It's him, isn't it? He's found us! What can we do?"

Berenko answered for me.

"Perhaps, Mr. Carter, it is time to drop our little charade. We have business to conduct, and covers can be cumbersome. We should move along with it, don't you agree?"

If he was trying to drive a wedge between myself and Robin, he certainly succeeded. Her eyes turned to me, blinking out her confusion. I was forced to agree with him. When I spoke to Robin again, all semblance of the phoney English accent was stripped from my voice.

"Look, Robin, my name is not McDaniel. It's Carter . . . Nick Carter. I'm with American Intelligence, and, at the moment, I'm working with Berenko. It is very important that you take us to whomever it is that gives you your orders."

Her body stiffened at the first mention of American Intelligence, and only grew harder as my speech continued.

"We need to find out more about your group. Something very big is going on in South Africa, it involves Nikumba, and we have to find out why your group is trying to kill him. You've got to help us."

To my surprise, Robin tore herself from my grasp. She stumbled backward, desperate for distance, her face and voice filling with venom.

"You son of a bitch!" she cried. "You lied to me! You bloody well lied to me! And to think I felt sorry for you! American Intelligence!"

She spoke the words as if she were choking on them.

"You're no better than he is!" she cried, her head jerking toward Berenko. "Russians, Americans, you're all the same to Africa. You bleed us, and run us, and use us as pawns in your sadistic little games of power!"

Berenko and I shared a look of amazement as she railed on.

"But not for long. The Society will rid us of you! It will rid us of your governments, your exploitation, your sickening ways of life. All of it will be swept away. Every trace of the white man's domination will be thrown out of Africa! And then, we'll rule ourselves . . . with African governments, built on African models . . . true to the African spirit!"

There was a moment's pause as Berenko and I tried to ingest her comments. I made an effort to reach through her hatred.

"Perhaps you're right, Robin," I said. "Maybe that's just what should happen. But we need to find out more about what you're talking about. We need to see what the Society is after. Perhaps we can help them."

"Bullshit!" came her reply.

There was more silence, then it was Berenko's turn for comment.

"The lady seems to have run out of words. Perhaps, Mr. Carter, your feelings are making you too gentle in this matter. It is quite possible that I can persuade the lady to offer her assistance."

Robin whirled on him. "Try it! You can kill me if you want, but you'll not get a word out of me. You can both go straight to hell for all I care!"

Berenko stared at me, awaiting either action or the

permission to work his own methods. The thought of Robin in Berenko's hands made my stomach churn.

The big Russian began advancing toward Robin. "In the field, my friend, there is no place for feelings. That remains the luxury of the world's normals . . . it is not for us to taste."

I was on the verge of agreement when the air came alive with sounds . . . mechanical sounds.

From behind one of the neighboring hangers came the roar of several engines, soon followed by the appearance of six military Jeeps. On top of this came the rumble of machinery as the hanger door we were facing suddenly rolled open, its light spilling across the runway and revealing the reflective nose of a Lear jet.

Our little group shared confusion as the Jeeps sped to a halt around us, each one depositing its cargo of soldiers . . . each soldier fully armed and focused on us.

We were surrounded, totally out-numbered, out-maneuvered, and out-gunned. Within seconds, all our weapons found their way to the ground. It was then that the sleek black limousine rounded the hangar and made its way to us.

Berenko and I exchanged a look of mutual frustration as a short, dignified looking man climbed out of the rear of the vehicle and approached us.

"Welcome," he chirped in crisp English. "You are looking for the Society of Nine, am I correct?"

Berenko and I both nodded mechanically.

"Well, then, your journey is at its end. If you will please follow me to the plane, I shall see that you are made comfortable."

"And just where might we be going?" I asked.

"To the home of the Society, Mr. Carter. This was your desire . . . yours and Mr. Berenko's . . . no? So shall it be. The leader wishes very much to meet and talk with both of you. With the young lady, also.'' He turned to face Robin. "You have served us very well, and now it is time for you to experience the rewards of your efforts.'' He extended his arm in a wide sweep toward the Lear. "If you would step this way, please? Just the three of you, if you don't mind. Your men, Mr. Berenko, will have to remain here. Certainly that is understandable?''

"So far, it's the only thing that is,'' Berenko growled.

No sooner had we stepped to the side, when gunfire burst behind us. Berenko and I both whipped around. On the tarmac were the four blasted bodies of Berenko's soldiers.

I threw him a glance. The jaws were tight as fists, and his eyes were narrowing in an effort to keep his rage from dominating him. But these were the only expressions he allowed. The rest was cool, total control.

"Your hospitality overwhelms me,'' he spat.

"My apologies,'' the man answered calmly. 'Now, if you will please follow me.''

The little man led the way as we filed in behind him. I worked my way over to Berenko, his face still carrying the tension within him. His eyes were glued to the man's neck, and I could feel his body readying for movement.

I had to distract him. We were in no position for action of any kind.

"Do I detect feelings, comrade?''

His head jerked toward me, and for a second I thought I might be the benefactor of his killing blow. And then it passed. With a release of breath his body relaxed, and the tension seemed to spill out over the runway.

"Yes, Mr. Carter, quite right.'' He gave a mirthless chuckle. "Feelings . . . feelings, indeed.''

We moved on together. The only remaining vestige of Berenko's hatred loosed itself in a whispered comment, just a few feet from the hangar entry.

"So we have found our game, Mr. Carter. We shall meet them, learn their purpose. And then, Mr. Carter . . . then we shall take them apart . . . yes?"

I turned and studied the small army around us. "No problem," I muttered. "I'll take care of the nineteen guns, you just keep the little guy in the suit off my back, okay?"

Berenko chuckled as we climbed onto the plane, both of us ready for our appointment with The Society of Nine.

CHAPTER TEN

The Society's home proved to be in the Comoro Islands, a tiny cluster of volcanic outcroppings off the eastern coast of Africa. The Society occupied a huge plantation complex on one of the smaller islands, Moheli.

We were definitely expected. We were escorted cordially to one of the plantation's basement conference rooms, with each new person we met greeting us by name.

The room itself was a study in primitive splendor. Its walls were decorated with tribal symbols and objects, while the floor was practically bare, possessing a series of mats for seating. At the end of the room stood a large dais, occupied with two ornately carved thrones.

Nine of the mats were occupied. It was the nature of these individuals that gave Berenko and me our first shock. These nine men were conspicuously familiar to both of us. A few represented key figures in Russian-run governments and resistance movements. The others represented democratic, or American-run countries.

On the world stage, these men would be clawing at each other, but somehow, in this room, they were as at home in each other's presence as alumni at a reunion.

A quick look at Berenko showed him to be as confused as I.

Suddenly a door at the far end of the room flew open, and in walked two figures. The first was obviously a man, but his features were obscured by a huge

leopard's mask. His upper torso was completely bare,
and his lower body covered only by a brightly colored
native skirt. Across his shoulders was draped a leopard
mantle that made him look every inch a king.

The other figure was female. She, too, wore only a
skirt, the full dimensions of her pendulous breasts
swinging unabashedly and proudly in front of her. She
too wore a mantle, but no mask. Her face was breath-
taking . . . a true African goddess . . . carved in dark
ebony, from the first thrust of her cheeks to the round,
sensual curve of her lips.

If these two were not royalty, the men in the room did
not know it. From the moment they came in, the nine
figures lowered themselves, their heads scraping the
floor and their chanting filling the room with sounds of
obedience and worship.

The two accepted this homage, finally calling it to a
halt as they took their positions on the thrones. From
nowhere, three chairs appeared behind us and we were
instructed to sit, Berenko to my left, and Robin to my
right.

For several moments the room remained silent. And
then the Black Goddess rose to address us.

"We welcome you to the home of the Society." Her
voice was rich and resonant, her speech in slightly
accented English. "You are, no doubt, curious as to
why you are here, and who we are."

It was a statement that needed no confirmation. Her
hand made an encompassing gesture as she continued.

"The nine men you see here are, I'm sure, as familiar to you as you are to them. Introductions would
therefore be superfluous. They are the inner council of
the Society of Nine. The Society represents an alliance
. . . very secret, and very strong . . . between nine
major South African countries."

As she listed them off, she would point to the particular individual representing that country.

"Angola, Botswana, Mozambique, Namibia, The Republic of South Africa, Rhodesia, Tanzania, Zaire, and finally Zambia.

"In each of these countries, the Society is comprised of key figures in government, the military, and the various industrial complexes. The men in this room head their respective organizations."

I could feel Berenko shifting in his seat beside me. "And to what purpose do they serve?" he ventured to the woman.

She stared at him a moment before answering. "All your questions will be addressed, Mr. Berenko. Until such time as you are given permission, you will please remain quite mute."

Berenko stiffened, but nodded his acquiescence.

The Goddess continued.

"The group's purpose is quite simple. To maintain a constant state of tension and warfare between *all* African countries, thereby assuring that all colonial or foreign forms of government remain unstable. When the time then comes that the Society feels it is ready to dominate, these governments will then be overthrown, and the nine countries involved will consolidate into one giant nation, built on African models.

"These particular nine countries represent the core of the group, since each is made up of primarily Bantu peoples. The Bantu culture will be the cornerstone from which the Society will build its African State. Once this consolidation is achieved, the smaller nations will fall quite naturally into our sphere of influence. It is fully believed by us that one day all of sub-Saharan Africa will exist as one large nation, with world minerals and resources as our private monopoly."

I whispered cautiously toward Berenko. "Maybe we

better get our tickets early. Looks like it's going to be a full house."

If he heard me, he ignored it. The Goddess still held center stage.

"The group is financed by all the monies channeled into these various countries by the U.S.A., Russia, the other colonial interests, and the mineral corporations. It is ironic, is it not? You all fight to have your own aims manifested, and the Society uses these goals, bolstering our own cause, feigning allegiances to yours . . . until that day when we shall rise up and throw you all out of Africa."

There was an almost maniacal tinge creeping into her voice.

"The group is huge, powerful, its members ranging from the giants of African freedom you see before you, to humble natives . . . all of whom wear the leopard tattoo . . . all dedicated to the sacred concept of Africa for Africans. Soon, very soon, we shall rid ourselves of the crushing weight of colonialism, and all Africa will merge into one giant Bantu nation!"

By this time, she had reached a peak of emotion. She towered to the full six feet of her statuesque body.

"And on that day, I shall reign as Anene, the Queen!" Suddenly she turned and faced her counterpart on his throne. "And M'Batti," she bellowed, "shall reign as the Leopard King!"

With this, she threw herself onto the floor. The room once more exploded into low, guttural rolls of chanting. To my shock, Robin moved from her seat and joined the others in their prostrate worship.

I looked over at Berenko. "Well," I whispered, "we seem to have discovered who they are and what they intend on doing. Any brilliant ideas as to how we're going to take them apart?"

"Patience, my friend," was his only reply.

Suddenly M'Batti stood up, silencing the room. The man was not particularly tall, but when he spoke, the room seemed to shake.

"The leopard shall devour the earth!"

This brought a rousing response from the assemblage. It didn't take me long to guess that the power of the man's voice was greatly aided by electronic boosters, probably a microphone hidden in the mask. If the others in the room noticed it, they kept it quite secret. He was working his minions with all the finesse of a circuit holy-roller.

The "leopard" chant ran on for minutes. As it reached the threshold of boredom, the man broke the spell by tossing off his mask.

Both Berenko and I sat bolt upright in our chairs. M'Batti was none other than Joseph Nikumba himself . . . live, and in the flesh.

I could hear Robin gasping for breath beside me. She leapt to her feet and ran to the man, sprawling herself out in front of him. She chattered almost maniacally, apologizing for all the things she had thought and said about the man. Not to mention the attempt on his life.

The room drifted into silence as the man answered her entreaties. Without the benefit of electronics, his voice was quite normal, almost fatherly in its gentleness.

"Do not feel badly, my child. You did as you were told to do. Nikumba is soon to be no more. M'Batti will take his place, and rule. You are a good soldier of the Society. Your work has helped to bring Africa's future into the present."

Robin was still horrified by her actions. "Why didn't you tell me? I could have made a mistake. Why didn't you let me know?"

Nikumba gently cupped her face in his hand. "No one is to know, child. That is our strength . . . secrecy! All soldiers of the Society, from the lowliest native to the very men in this room, are kept purposely ignorant of the greater purposes of the Society. All know only one thing . . . Africa for Africans!''

The room made as if to respond, but Nikumba cut them off with a raise of his hand.

''The true purposes of the Society are known only to myself and Anene. All others are fed what little information they need to operate, and always in terms that fit their own given philosophies and motives. In this way, we can deal with and manipulate the countries and interests that oppress us, both on their terms and seemingly to their benefit.''

Like the Goddess before him, Nikumba's fatherly manner was slowly giving way to an insane kind of energy as his speech built in intensity.

''In public, our members fight each other in the name of Communism, or Democracy. On the battle fields, Society soldier kills Society soldier, all holding the cause in their hearts, waiting for that day when we can rise up, together, and claim what is ours!'' Both arms raised high above his head, fists clenched. ''And that time is *now!*''

The man was rolling.

''Take honor, child! Take honor in having brought to us the instruments of that great revolution!''

With this, one hand flew out in the direction of Berenko and myself. Whatever part we were to play, it was as unclear to Robin as to us.

''But, I didn't bring them. They forced me to lead them to you. I was to return alone . . . those were my orders. And I failed.''

Nikumba answered her, but stared intently at us in the process.

''You were meant to fail. Both men's skills are well known. Both you and Bosima were assigned because you are not professionals, as they are. You were both possessing of weaknesses, and it was *because* of those weaknesses you were chosen. We wanted them to realize our existence. We wanted them to join forces and make their way to us. They are the vehicles of liberation!''

Nikumba turned and faced her.

''Your weakness, child, was our strongest ally!''

Then he turned and delivered the finale to the room in general. ''There is great honor in what you have done. The moment of Africa's rebirth is at hand! These men will throw their countries into a battle of accusation and counter-accusation that will tear the white man's world to pieces! And then we shall rise . . . nine into one . . . to solidify Southern Africa, then *all* of Africa, and finally . . .''

His voice was at a complete emotional crescendo as he screamed out the final words.

''AND FINALLY, THE WORLD ITSELF! THE LEOPARD SHALL DEVOUR THE EARTH!''

The assembly roared its approval.

''The man's crazy,'' Berenko gasped. ''Stark raving mad!''

In the middle of the commotion, both Nikumba and his Queen strode regally from the room. Within seconds, we were being escorted after them. I shot a quick look to Robin. She looked helpless, trying to absorb the enormity of all she had been confronted with. I felt for her . . . a little girl, suddenly caught up in a very big game.

We were shoved through the doors to the more humble surroundings of a simple office. Behind the desk sat Nikumba, flanked on his right and left by the towering figures of two Watusi. Obviously, the palace guard.

''Impressive, are they not?'' Nikumba smiled.

"Watusi's, the elite of African manhood, and far more skilled and able than the three you dealt with in Algiers, Mr. Carter. Of that, I assure you!"

A low rumble from the floor to my right diverted my attention away from the glowering black giants.

I couldn't keep a gasp from erupting from my throat as I watched two hundred and fifty pounds of live leopard rise from his corner of the room and begin gliding toward us, his amber eyes studying our every move.

Nikumba laughed delightedly. "And this is Vadu, my pet and watchdog. A very cooperative and very loyal friend, gentlemen." Suddenly he barked out a command, and the animal flew at us. There was shared horror, and then relief as the cat was stopped, inches short of us, by a leash of thick cording.

"We get the message, Nikumba," I said, my voice anything but calm.

His look grew stern. "Nikumba is no more, gentlemen. I am M'Batti, and that is how you will please address me."

We both grunted our acceptance. His face brightened at our concession. With another brief command, he summoned the leopard back to the corner. Then he stood and paced, certain that his bodyguards would discourage any action on our parts. Berenko and I did our best to regain composure.

"How? Is that not the question lodged now in your minds? How will this African Renaissance occur?"

The question was rhetorical, so we merely waited out the answer.

"The answer begins with your country, Mr. Carter. The American negotiations that have finally put black rule into South Africa. The announcement, as a matter of fact, was made this morning. Joseph Nikumba is to head an interim council, for the express purpose of forming a black government. Upon the completion of this process, the government will then be voted on, and all expect it to be accepted with great enthusiasm. Nikumba shall be South Africa's first black leader. Telegrams have been pouring in, gentlemen. The African world is ecstatic at the good fortunes of our efforts.''

''And just how does that affect us?'' I asked.

M'Batti smiled. ''It puts, as you know, your country into a very dangerous political posture. Although America is to be commended on its courage, the Namibia question is a delicate one . . . one an intelligent government would do best to avoid.''

''So if we're not happy after thirty days, we'll send it back, okay?''

He continued, unruffled by my sarcasm.

''You'll have to forgive us, Mr. Carter, but we took the liberty of leaking this delicate information to the Soviet Union. After all, they too have their concerns.''

It was Berenko's turn. ''Your generosity is as baffling as your motives. Please, do continue.''

Again the comment was taking in stride. Nikumba/M'Batti had the irritating confidence of someone who knows they're going to win.

''Ah, yes. The motives. The sequence you already know. Two doubles, carefully executed, for the sole purpose of attracting two rather well-known agents into Africa.''

It was my turn again. ''Why didn't you just send an engraved invitation? My social calendar was quite empty.''

Nothing could get to him. ''Sequence!'' he barked, his finger jabbing the air. ''We needed for both of you to follow certain patterns of behavior, and certain routes through Africa. Invitations would never have sufficed. You see, gentlemen, we needed certain bits of proof and documentation. We needed a record . . . in photographs, in video tapes, in sound recordings, of two of the super-powers' most able operatives in action!''

Berenko hissed. ''You flatter us.''

''Not at all. The two of you were most cooperative. We have amassed an excellent collection of films and recordings . . . a veritable volume of travel information. In short, a very convincing diary of two agents in action.''

My turn. ''So sell it to Hollywood, you'll make a killing.''

The man had the gall to actually laugh.

''I'm not sure you would like to see the private encounters of you and Robin spread across the giant screen, Mr. Carter.''

For a second I saw red. My body jolted, and tensed. M'Batti's leopard must have sniffed it, because he moved suddenly in toward his master. I took one look at those fangs glistening beneath those snarling lips, and let the moment pass. I settled back in my chair.

Berenko moved in. ''And to what purpose have you gone to all this trouble, Mr. M'Batti?''

''A story,'' he answered. ''We needed to tell a story. It is an interesting story, and you two are the central figures in it. All your movements and actions since you first arrived in Africa have been duly recorded. The interesting thing about this story is that, although you gentlemen know why and what you were doing, the rest of the world . . . does not!''

His face broke into an evil grin.

''Contrary to popular belief, pictures *do* lie, gentlemen! Taken out of context and out of sequence, pictures of one series of events can be quite easily be made to tell a different story, a complete distortion of the truth of events.''

A queasy feeling was beginning to gather in the depths of my belly.

''Picture it, gentlemen! Two espionage agents, so thinly disguised as to be transparent, making their way through Africa, leaving in their wakes the shattered corpses of all who would stand in their way, both with the single-minded goal of achieving their missions. Perhaps you were right after all, Mr. Carter. It is a powerful vehicle for the movies!''

''Care to give us a libretto?'' I growled.

''Delighted!'' he chirped. ''As I mentioned earlier, Nikumba has been named to form a government for South Africa. It is a brilliant choice, as I'm sure you both agree, but there is one small drawback. Tomorrow, Joseph Nikumba is going to be assassinated.''

Berenko and I exchanged looks. M'Batti ignored us. He began pacing the room as he unfolded his twisting of events.

''The world, of course, will be horrified, even appalled. Inquiries will be made, and over the next week or so, a story will begin to emerge. A very sad, sad story indeed. A tragic death!

''The story goes something like this. Joseph Nikumba and the American government have entered into secret negotiations for the establishment of a black ruled government in South Africa. A successful formula is reached, and emotions begin climbing as the white leaders see a possible solution to their political dilemmas. The United States is, however, taking a rather risky position on the question of Namibia; but, for that they can be forgiven. Black rule, after all, is the *real* issue; one small lapse of judgment can be overlooked.''

I nodded. "I'll give your solicitations to Uncle Sam."

"Indeed, Mr. Carter, indeed." He was just too smug for comfort. "And what happens now? The Soviet Union learns of these events, and sees it as a direct conflict to *their* interests in Namibia. None other than Yuri Berenko himself, enters the field!"

Berenko refrained from comment. He just studied the floor, sifting everything through his agile brain.

"And what does Mr. Berenko do? The thing any good operative would do. He finds a way to get to Nikumba!"

"May I?" asked Berenko. M'Batti nodded his assent. "So, in an effort to reach you, I begin manipulating your wife. All thoroughly documented, of course. Her leftist leanings are not a secret. I merely play on those leanings, bending her to my own cause and purpose."

"Indeed you did, Mr. Berenko. That, and more! Not satisfied with just getting information from her, you began twisting her against her husband, using her as leverage against him. Under such duress, Nikumba was forced to meet with you, to bend to some of your demands."

"But," said Berenko with almost a note of victory. "This is not documented. We never met, Mr.—excuse me! Nikumba and I never met!"

"This is true," the man laughed. "But Nikumba and your double did. Several times. You begin to see just how deceiving the camera can be, yes?"

Victory gave way to defeat. "I'm beginning to."

"So to continue, gentlemen, meetings occur between Nikumba and Berenko. And what happens then? America learns of it, and starts to fear that treachery may be brewing. Information is suddenly uncovered by them, confirming Nikumba as a Russian puppet. I'm sure, Mr. Carter, that this sudden discovery of information is familiar to you from your reports back to base, yes?''

''It does ring a bell.''

''And how does America react? They send in one of their first-rate assassins to determine the nature of things.''

It was my turn to spot a hole, and taste the victory.

''One problem there, M'Batti. I was already in Africa when the news was reached. Working a little out of sequence, aren't you?''

He shook his head remorsefully. ''It is not yet clear to you, is it, Mr. Carter. *You* know that. *I* know that. Mr. Berenko knows that. The story is a *lie, Mr. Carter!* But the world does NOT know that! There are just pictures, Mr. Carter, and the world will see what we want them to!''

I had to keep trying. ''And what of the dates, the travel records? Those *are* in sequence, they're recorded.''

He laughed. ''You mean dates on the car *we* rented in Algiers? The charter flight *we* set up? The jet *we* provided? We hold the paper on those transactions, and I promise you, they are in total harmony with our purposes. And just to show you how careless you can be, Mr. Carter, on the few things you did sign, did you think to check the dates listed? What was the date on the bill of lading at the shippers when you picked up your arsenal?''

There was no answer. I accepted defeat as gracefully as possible.

''So, to get on with events. Mr. Carter is shipped into Africa, and he too, like all good agents, tries to find his leverage on Nikumba. And what happens? He begins preying on a young, beautiful Nikumba aide, who is harmlessly vacationing in Algiers. The girl takes to him. They even vacation across North Africa together. And, woe unto her, she falls a helpless victim to love. The evil Mr. Carter sinks in his hooks and draws the young victim into his web of conspiracy. Aren't you the least bit ashamed, Mr. Carter?''

"You think it'll kill my chances at the pearly gates?" I quipped.

For the first time, M'Batti looked halfway serious. "You may know the answer to that sooner than you care to."

We eyeballed each other for a second, before the smile returned to his face.

"So, Mr. Carter and his young sparrow make their way to Windhoek. Nikumba is to make a speech, probably one of the most brilliant of his career. If you hadn't both been so busy that day, I think you would have appreciated it. What the world heard that day was a stunning new concept. Nikumba, who had so successfully built up the model for bringing African tribes together, was now unveiling a new model. A model for East-West detente. A model for cooperative involvement, both by America *and* Russia, in the newly emerging black South African Nation. A model that all other third world nations might adopt, to lessen the friction of world tension!''

"A pity," Berenko commented, turning to me. "With all that peace and harmony, what would we find to do on weekends?"

"Don't worry," I answered. "It'll never get through the Senate."

For the first time, M'Batti/Nikumba began to show reaction.

"I have the feeling you gentlemen are not taking me seriously. That is your business. The world, I assure you, will."

"Just trying to keep our spirits up," I offered.

"Please, may I fill in a chapter or two?"

M'Batti nodded his assent.

"The way I figure it, the world is duly impressed with yet another mental achievement on the part of Nikumba. But, behind the scenes, those incredible Society informers have been feeding the U.S.A. more information. The Nikumba Plan is not what it appears. It is meant to sound like an East-West package, only to put us off our guard. What it really is, is a first step toward calming the masses to a Russian presence. Later on, when things begin to settle with the new government, the brilliant new detente will begin swinging more toward the East than the West, until, somewhere down the road, the Russians own the whole ball game and America is out on its ass. Correct?"

The smile was back. "Yes! Excellent, Mr. Carter. That is it, exactly! And that is why you tried to kill me, you see. Fortunately for me, Mr. Berenko stopped you."

"And what if I hadn't stopped him?"

M'Batti faced Berenko. "I have a doctorate in psychology, Mr. Berenko. I know the human animal very well. Spies are a unique breed, but common nonetheless. Your presence here alone is testimony to my abilities at predicting your behaviors. But that aside, I leave nothing to chance. If there are doubles for you, gentlemen, you can be certain that there is a double for me."

Berenko bowed in mock admiration.

"But, I am anxious to get on with our story, gentlemen! The American plan is risky, but daring. The attempt is to be covered with some story about a Liam McDaniel . . . white, colonial racist. There is even evidence that England will enter this plot by providing a body. The Queen will take a dim view of that, no doubt."

"No doubt," I added.

"But, all turns out well. Mr. Berenko makes a daring rescue. The culprit and his hapless aide are transported to the Russian embassy, and all looks well for Nikumba."

"One question," I interjected. "Berenko ordered my capture, and loaded up his soldiers with tranquilizers. Bosima, however, retained her poison, quite intent on my death. How do you explain that?"

His face flushed for just the smallest second. "My apologies, Mr. Carter. Even a Doctor of Psychology can err. It seems that sometimes we misjudge the emotions and drives of those closest to us far more than we do the comparative stranger. Her zeal in the pursuit of her mission took on greater proportions than at first realized. She had paid for it."

"Your own wife!" Berenko hissed.

M'Batti checked him. "A soldier, Mr. Berenko! A soldier for a cause! But we digress. We must pick up the story, yes? So, Mr. Berenko has removed the threat to his embassy. But, lo and behold, the wily Mr. Carter escapes . . . with his poor aide in tow. My special admiration, Mr. Carter, on the quality of the escape. The films of your crashing into the limousine would do justice to the violence of your weekly television shows."

"It's a little known secret," I answered. "I got my license in a lottery."

As usual, he ignored me.

"It is here, gentlemen, that the record of Mr. Carter's activities gets sketchy. There are the bodies of three S.W.A.P.O. guerrillas to mark his exit from Angola. Later there will be the body of Robin, the poor, victimized aide, to mark his entry into Zaire."

Involuntarily, I jumped. Once more the leopard moved, reading anger in my body, and running the full length of his leash. One giant paw lashed out, shaving hairs off the back of my hand. M'Batti stared at me, daring me to make another step.

"You seem upset, Mr. Carter. Take some consolation in the fact that she will die in the country of her birth. The soil of the Congo shall reclaim its own."

The man was quickly earning my hatred. He had clearly established his dominance, both physical and mental, over the situation. With a clipped command he called the big cat off. I settled back again, rolling through my mind just how many ways I could kill him when the time came.

He continued. "There you have it, gentlemen. Tomorrow, Nikumba is to address an assembly of gleeful Zairans, in the capitol city of Kinshasa. He will be sharing with them their joy over the new government-to-be, and further revealing details of his innovative East-West approach. You, Mr. Berenko, are even going to be on the stand to introduce him!"

I looked to the Russian, but there was no response.

"But, tragedy will mar this sublime celebration. Against all odds, you, Mr. Carter, are going to finally succeed in your mission. To even further shroud events, both you, Mr. Carter, and you, Mr. Berenko, will add your bodies to the list of dead, during the aftermath.

"From here, events will spiral out of control. On information provided by us, the world will come to learn of this horrifying sequence of events. America will be publicly castigated, your own country, Mr. Berenko, no doubt being the first on the bandwagon."

Berenko could not suppress a chuckle. "Indeed, M'Batti. America will be in great disgrace. Perhaps we can compensate you for your success."

M'Batti's energy was beginning to soar. "Save your

ruples, Mr. Berenko. You will need them. We cannot leave our American comrades in such a dire situation. They will need a counter attack, and we shall provide one.

"A new Russian posture will suddenly, and conveniently, begin to emerge. When Nikumba's plan failed to please your government, you began to exert even greater pressures, Mr. Berenko. Nikumba's wife, once cooperative, now becomes a prisoner in your embassy. You use her presence there to blackmail Nikumba into making swifter, and more anti-American, progress in his speeches. And then, an accident. Bosima is killed. The photos of your embassy extermination team in operation will tear the heart out of a grieving world."

It was Berenko's turn to jolt. The leopard showed no preference for political idiologies. He lunged until called off by M'Batti. This was the only break in the man's rapidly mounting narrative.

"Yes, Mr. Berenko, a regrettable error, but one duly covered and withheld from poor Nikumba. Assuming his wife to still be alive, he agrees to your terms. The Kinshasa speech is rewritten by you to expose the American danger. It is your plan to have Nikumba feign fear for his life at the revelation. At which point, you were to offer him your protection until he could safely return to South Africa."

Berenko's face was coloring a bright red as he spat out out his words. "And what that means is that Russia will stage a few American purges from its groups in South Africa. In the meantime, we will subject Nikumba to the cruelest of brainwashing techniques. Just enough to regain the leverage his wife's death deprived us of. And then, when all is ready, we return to South Africa, triumphant."

"Exactly! Unfortunately for you, Mr. Carter's skills

prove too great, and the plans of all concerned die with the termination of Nikumba. And that, gentlemen, is all the Society will need!''

His voice was rumbling. His eyes glowed, and the patter of his speech mounted in the holy-roller fashion he had displayed earlier.

''The world will be horrified at the chain of events. Two powers, competing and interfering in foreign territories for their own petty interests, are willing to ignore world opinion and the sanctity of human life in the blind pursuit of those goals! A single black leader, a gentle professor of world peace, is blackmailed by Russia, and killed by America. His wife murdered, his world policies twisted by interference. Joseph Nikumba will rise up to become the greatest black martyr that Africa has ever known!''

Berenko and I just sat, the certainty of his claims chilling us to our souls.

''In the weeks that follow, Africans from across the continent . . . some of them pawns in your stupid games . . . all of them with tattoos on their bellies will suddenly find unity in the image of Joseph Nikumba. Enemies will join hands in friendship, following the models of tribal unity Nikumba so graciously gave the world. But! They will not throw down their arms! They will turn them instead on the white man . . . any white man . . . anywhere he exists! They will unite to rid Africa of its cancerous infestation! The blood of the African white man will fertilize the African soil in this spring of its rebirth!''

By now, the man was gone. His body was quivering. His eyes were burning into both of us. I was not completely certain that we were not going to find ourselves the first installment on his payments of blood.

To my relief, he broke from us, moving toward the curtained wall on our left. He tore open the curtains, and revealed to us the final ingredients in his stew of African conquest.

"There, gentlemen! It is they who will play out the final chapter in my scenario!"

Too much had been thrown at me. Try as I might, I couldn't even muster an expression of modest surprise.

Behind a thick glass partition sat three men. Joseph Nikumba, Yuri Berenko, and yours truly. A trio of perfect doubles just waiting their chance to write history.

"Once they have completed their part, the same plastic surgeon who created them, and the two that drew you in, will then give me a new face . . . M'Batti's face . . . the face that will lead and rule the new Bantu Empire!"

Berenko looked over at me, his expression as limp as my own. I could see the pain in his eyes. He shook his head briefly, then spoke, his words sounding like an epitaph in the wake of Nikumba's bellowing.

"The leopard shall devour the Earth."

CHAPTER ELEVEN

Berenko and I were prisoners in the basement of the Society complex. The room had apparently once been a wine cellar or larder of some kind. We were entirely surrounded by stone, and yet there was a warmth to the room; almost as though it were centrally heated, its pipes tied into the cauldron of volcanic fluids that churned beneath the island.

It was our spirits that were damp, and chilled.

We both sat on cots, lost in the depths of our own thoughts. I studied him. The single bulb in the room was reflecting off the big Russian's glasses, giving him almost a "Little Orphan Annie" quality. But what his eyes would not give up, his body did.

Misery was our silent cell-mate.

I knew that action was called for, and quickly, before we immersed ourselves in debilitating self-pity.

"Berenko?"

He looked toward me. With the movement of his head, his eyes were once more visible. They clearly showed his pain.

"I have something to ask you, and I don't want you to think I'm crazy, okay?"

He waited.

"Does the sun ever shine in Russia?"

His bushy brows furrowed in temporary confusion, then a smile broke out on his lips. "Yes, my friend. Sometimes. With incredible brilliance. But, you see, the problem is that Russia is a huge nation, and to light it all would burn the sun out in a week. So the Politburo, in all its wisdom, has ruled that the sun shall light the country in sections, each comrade getting his fair share in shifts. *That,* my friend, is Communism in action!''

With the sounds of our laughter, misery fled. It was the release we both needed. In its wake, came the action we both felt comfortable with.

Berenko leaned forward on his cot. ''We are in a bad position,'' he said. ''It is strange. Our two countries push and shove at one another in a game of verbal battle that, too often, threatens to ignite. And now, suddenly, from outside this arena comes a group with all the tools necessary to bury us. It seems that sometimes we focus so intently on one another, that we forget others are capable of moving events.''

''They must be stopped!'' I hissed.

''Yes,'' he nodded, ''but our freedom is somewhat limited at the moment. Assuming escape, what are our options in this matter?''

I rose and began pacing the cell. ''Obviously, the first move would be to stop the assassination. Without a body, there is no martyr, and their information becomes worthless. They would have to shelve it.''

''They could rig another attempt.''

''Sure, they could, but that would call for more doubles, and that would take time. Some of their secrecy is now shot. We know the identities of the inner council. If we could neutralize them, before a second attempt can be constructed, then the organization would collapse.''

Berenko shook his head. ''I think that's too risky, and not firm enough. They must have fall-back plans in case of failure. No, we must get hold of Nikumba. We must control the brain. If we do that, the body will follow.''

''But how? He'll never cooperate on his own, and if

we kill him, even if we aren't caught doing it, the evidence they have would come right back off the shelf, and convict us.''

A slow, cunning smile spread over Berenko's lips. "The double, my friend, the *double!*''

"What?''

"The double was on the podium in Windhoek. *He* spoke! *He* delivered the speech, and no one knew it wasn't Nikumba. If we can get the Nikumba double into our hands, and then eliminate M'Batti, I'm convinced we can pressure the double into saying anything we want him to!''

"Berenko, you Ruskie bastard, you're brilliant!''

"Of course, my friend,'' he chuckled. "Now, let's follow this through all its possibilities. We would have to kill both of our own doubles. Then I would take the stand with Nikumba's alternate. We would stop the assassination, but not the attempt. You could fire off a few shots, just enough to create a panic. During which, I could kidnap the bogus Nikumba.''

We were now both up and pacing the room.

"And we'd still have my cover story from Windhoek!'' I said. "We could resurrect the McDaniel, white racist theme, produce the body of my double . . . unrecognizable, of course . . . and get full corroboration from Harcourt and British Intelligence.''

Berenko laughed. "England strikes a blow for black rule. My God, they'll come out looking like heroes!''

"In the meantime, we go to work on the double. We make sure he continues his East-West formula of cooperation. We throw our full weight behind it, and suddenly America and Russia are the angels of African harmony.''

"The plot completely collapses!'' chirped Berenko.

"Not only that,'' I added. "But with Nikumba—the *supposed* Nikumba, that is—is our control, the Society is all but frozen. We then start putting the heat on the inner nine, and from there, just work our way down the ladder.''

Berenko leaped toward me and slapped his hands on my shoulders. "Do you see it?" he cried. I wasn't entirely sure I did.

"The secrecy!" he bellowed. "That secrecy that M'Batti was so safe with. Suddenly it would be our biggest ally. M'Batti and Anene are the only two who know the full workings and plans of the Society. With them gone, there is no future.''

Suddenly catching the drift, I burst in. "And the present is only understood by the inner council. With them eliminated, the soldiers of the Society would just plod along, motivated only by the *mis*information M'Batti and his henchmen had fed them.''

"Exactly!" Berenko was almost triumphant. "We need go no farther than the leaders of the Society. With them eliminated, beliefs will remain as diversified as ever, and the world remains quite status quo!''

The ideas were appearing like magic. For a few, precious moments, the world was alive again. There was light at the end of the tunnel.

But there was also, however, a big, locked iron gate.

The planning was sound, *if* we could escape. *If* we could get to Kinshasa in time. *If* we could neutralize our doubles. *If* we could get M'Batti and Anene. And if we had a small army to help us.

Together we searched the walls of the room, using the years of experience to try and find that one chink in the armor. One loose stone was found and pried loose, only to reveal the hard-packed earth that signified our position as firmly underground.

Time ruled out any tunnels.

Direct assault was all that was left us. Quickly, Berenko unscrewed the overhead light. I crouched in a corner where I could see the door, and Berenko stationed himself behind it. When the guards showed up, we would be waiting for them.

Nearly a half hour passed before we heard the rattle of keys. We tensed, every nerve in our bodies readied for action and commands, and then the door flew open.

Whoever the guard was, the darkness held him in the hall. And then, with careful, timid steps the figure moved into the room. Berenko was crouched, with his shoulder to the door, waiting for a shout from me to take the guard.

I watched for the appearance of a weapon, holding my orders until the best chance for getting the gun revealed itself. But there was no gun. Instead there were frail, delicate hands, followed by the body I had come to know so well.

Robin became visible in the harsh back-light from the hall.

"Berenko, freeze!" I yelled.

Robin followed the sound of my voice and ran over to me once the dim outline of my body became visible to her. As I wrapped her in my arms, Berenko moved in to re-screw the bulb.

"What in the hell are you doing here?" I asked.

"I have to leave for Kinshasa. I didn't want to leave without seeing you."

"Where's the jailor?"

"In the adjoining room . . . the guard room."

Berenko and I both made for the door.

"No!" she cried. "There are four of them in there, and they have rifles. They're watching the corridor. You wouldn't get three steps down the hall before they'd cut you to pieces!"

I turned on her. "Is Nikumba, or M'Batti, or whatever the hell he calls himself, still here?"

She shook her head no. "He left an hour ago. I'm to fly out on a second plane and join him in Kinshasa."

"Robin, you were in that room. You've got to know the man is insane. Why are you continuing to work with him?"

"It's just enthusiasm," she replied coolly, her manner full of resolve. "I admit the room surprised me, even frightened me a little, but that's just an image he's trying to project. Later, when victory has been achieved, the real Nikumba will return."

"Bullshit!" I hissed. I tried my best to quickly explain M'Batti's plans to her, giving her a run-down of what the man was going to loose on the world, once his own death had been artfully achieved. "Robin, you've got to help us!"

"Nick," she cried, "it'll change! He'll do what is right, I know it. Africa will be free!"

It was just so many years of indoctrination talking, and I knew it. But we needed her help. I had to burst her bubble and make her see the truth.

"He'll do what's right?" I asked.

"Yes!"

"And you back it, all the way, no matter what measures he takes?"

"Yes!"

"Good," I said coolly. "Then you've just accepted your own death!"

She was stunned into silence. Before her defenses could rally, I bombarded her with the part of M'Batti's plot that called for Robin's body as final tribute to my supposedly self-interested planning.

When I had finished, she was unable to reply. Her head just kept wagging back and forth, refusing to accept the truth of my words.

"He's mad, Robin, you've got to see that. Your

death means nothing to him, father or not. He needs *you* to be the capper on his little movie.''

And still the head shook.

"Why aren't you on the plane with him, right now?"

She had no answer, so I supplied one.

"Because you can't be seen with him. Because no one can see you get off that plane. Because the world will soon learn that you are already dead in Kinshasa."

"No!" she cried.

"No?" I echoed. "Who the hell are you flying out with?"

"The guards," she replied, shakily. "The guards in the other room."

"Oh, that's sweet. They'll just escort you to Kinshasa. They'll feed you coffee, tea or milk all the way, and then carry you on a litter to daddy Nikumba's suite, right?"

"He wanted me to rest. He said I'd done tremendous service to the cause, and he wanted me to rest."

"You'll rest, all right. No sooner do you lift off in that plane, than they'll quietly put you to sleep, forever. The body will be mournfully rushed to whatever hideaway in Kinshasa that M'Batti has chosen as your grave. The world will mourn, and Robin will have completed her duty to Africa."

Robin's hands were trying to cover her ears. The tears were pouring. It was hard for me to batter her, but nowhere near as hard as letting M'Batti/Nikumba win.

She took it as long as she could. I had no room for subtlety, and she finally cracked under the barrage of my comments.

"You've got to believe me!" I cried.

"Why? You lied to me. You lied then, and you're lying now!" With that, she raced from the room, slamming the door behind her and locking it firmly.

I looked to Berenko. If he found fault with the way I

had just handled things, he was merciful in not sharing it with me.

He touched my arm briefly. "You tried."

With that, he returned to the bulb, unscrewed it, and both of us found our way to our original positions.

Again, the moments dragged their feet. Again, the door sounded an entry. And, to my surprise, again it was Robin.

I halted Berenko. Robin stood in the door, her body a statement of misery. I moved quickly to her, took her into my arms, and squeezed.

"You're going to help us?"

She nodded yes.

"Why?"

She looked at me with eyes so miserable, I wanted to melt.

"I went upstairs to get my things. I was trying to tell myself that you were lying, that Nikumba was not mad, that you were using me. I was almost convinced. I was within a hair's breadth of hating you. I *had* to!"

I nodded, and stroked her face as she finished.

"And then I saw him."

"Who?" I asked.

"You! He was *you!*" Her body was shaking. "But it wasn't you. When I saw him, all my resolve crumbled. All my hate dropped out of me, and I almost ran to him. And then he did it!"

"Did what?"

Her words traveled out in whimpers. "He had the gun, the one you used in Windhoek. He was laughing and joking with the guards. When he saw me start toward him, he froze. And then, he smiled . . . not your smile . . . a horrible, evil smile. He nudged one of the guards, winked, and leveled the gun, right in my face."

I gripped her harder as she cried on.

"He made a noise . . . a silly noise, and acted as though the gun had just gone off. I didn't know what to do. I just stood there staring at him. And then the guards laughed. Oh, Nick, they *are* going to kill me!"

"Not if I can help it, baby," I said, then released her and held her at arm's length. "We haven't got time to waste, Robin. What's the situation in the complex?"

She steeled herself and jumped miraculously into action. "There's only a skeleton guard remaining. Most of the forces are with M'Batti. Two of the guards have already left for the hangar with your double. I stalled the other two. They're waiting for me outside with a second car."

I looked to Berenko. He gave me a small smile and a nod, showing his appreciation of Robin's abilities. I turned back to her. "What about the guard room?"

"Only one man," she said. "And I have already taken care of him. The remainder of the guard will either be asleep, or out on the perimeters. When Nikumba leaves, the guards get very lax. Follow me!"

She led us down the hall to the guard room. There, behind a desk, sat the only guard, his body stretched back in his chair, and a silver brooch protruding from his neck. I made a silent promise to myself, never again to trust any woman who wore jewelry.

Robin for the moment, seemed to be totally in charge. She pointed toward the dead soldier, barking her commands.

"He's about your size, Nick. Get into his uniform."

The logic of it escaped me.

"I don't understand," I protested. "Nikumba's guard is black. How the hell are we going to fool anyone in uniforms?"

"Just the inner guard . . . the Watusis . . . and a few others. Most of his personal body guards are re-cruited from white mercenaries. It's a move he made to try to quell the white's fears. The uniform will make it easier for us to take the car upstairs, and the plane at the airport.''

I began stripping the guard as she continued.

"The uniforms will also make it easier for you to maneuver around the speech site tomorrow.''

"What about Berenko?" I asked.

"He can get a uniform off one of the guards at the car.''

Berenko's voice broke in as I began donning my new outfit.

"What about the body?''

"The guard won't change until eight o'clock in the morning,'' Robin answered. "The bodies won't be discovered until then.''

"Good,'' I said. "That'll buy us the time to get to Kinshasa. When's the speech?''

"At eleven.''

Berenko and I looked at each other. If the bodies were discovered at eight, there would still be three hours for the Society legions to let Nikumba know that all was not well on the homefront. The odds weren't great, but they were all we had. Berenko shrugged, reading my thoughts. We'd just have to hope the home guard was careless, or the communications with Kinshasa, painfully slow.

"We'll need weapons,'' the Russian growled. "Where can we get them?''

Robin was already ahead of him. She led us down one of the basement corridors to an armory. Berenko and I both froze at the sight of it. Either the man was petrified of being caught off guard, or he was planning to arm the whole of Africa on his own. The room contained an assortment of weapons that would make an army's mouth water.

Much to my delight, Robin walked straight to a

counter and handed me Wilhelmina and Hugo. Berenko also found his gun. We then ransacked the place, careful to select the small arsenal of automatic weapons we would need in our tiny commando force.

For the sake of concealment, we chose three well-oiled Sten guns, and enough ammunition to function economically. A few silencers finished the shopping list.

As I stuffed the pockets of my uniform full of goodies, I suddenly noticed a door at the end of one of the aisles. I moved over, and using Hugo picked open the antiquated lock.

It was a bonanza.

On the other side of the door was a small room, loaded to the ceiling with high explosives. It was hard to keep the triumph from my voice.

"I think I just bought us our three hours!"

One look and Berenko caught my drift. Together, we moved into the room and broke open one of the cases of plastique. Removing my A.X.E. issue wristwatch, I withdrew two tiny lead wires, concealed within the watch's multi-purpose casing. I set the alarm for 8:05, five minutes after guard change, and left the watch to do its job.

At exactly 8:05, the alarm would go off, hitting the plastique with a deceptively active current that would ignite the explosives. By the look of the boxes in the room, the resultant blast would blow the island off the face of the globe. It was very unlikely that anyone would be doing any communicating with Kinshasa after that.

We arrived at the airport with little to hinder us. Taking the two guards awaiting Robin at the car had been simple, and silent. The uniforms had done their job. It wasn't until we were on them that the two goons suspected anything amiss. By then, it was too late.

The hangar was a different story.

A quick surveillance through the hangar's windows told us we were in for a fight. The hangar was huge and well lit, with little inside to use as cover. Once through the entry doors, it would be only seconds before our unfamiliarity was spotted.

Inside were three of the guards, and the two-man crew who were to fly the plane. They were relaxed, and intently involved in conversation. That left one guard and the Nick double unaccounted for. We had to assume they were already on the plane.

The hangar doors stood wide open in preparation for departure. The only other entry would be one small door in the wall, directly opposite the entry ladder to the plane.

Berenko and I both agreed that our uniforms would get us nowhere. Direct assault was our only hope.

"But how?" I asked. "It's at least a three man show. Two guns would have to come in through the hangar doors, and a third would have to get to the plane before the two inside have a chance to seal it off. Without the plane we'll never get to Kinshasa, and it would be too easy for someone inside to radio for reinforcements."

"You're forgetting, Nick. There *are* three of us," Robin said quietly, taking the Stein from my hands. "What is it you want me to do?"

The plan was formulated as silencers found their way to the muzzles of the rifles. It was decided that Robin and Berenko would take the open doors, doing their best to keep the crew alive. It would be up to me to take the side door and seal off the plane's interior.

We all assumed our positions.

Berenko waited for the best moment. The crew

moved off to the wall to pick up their flight bags, and Robin and Berenko then burst in on the guards.

At the first sound of fire, I pumped Wilhelmina into the latch securing the side door, and kicked it open. The first burst was all that Berenko needed to level the guard. I raced through the door and rushed the Lear, taking the steps to the hatch two at a time.

Guard number four was struggling with the hatch. I slammed into the half-closed door and drove him back against the opposite wall. I threw myself after him, careful to clear the opening to the aisle as quickly as possible, just in case my double had firepower.

I pinned the luckless guard against the curved wall of the aircraft, and in three quick chops, put him quietly to sleep.

I then planted myself to the wall, trying to decide the next step. I listened intently for the lightest sounds of movement. All I could hear was Robin and Berenko rounding up the crew, persuading them to assist us.

I had to move. I had two choices. He could be in the cockpit, but that seemed the lesser of the two possibilities. He had to be in the cabin. There was enough certainty on my part to gamble.

I dropped into the aisle, Wilhelmina poised toward the plane's rear. The aisle was deserted.

He was back there somewhere, I could feel it.

I rose slowly, and began moving toward the back. Every instinct was seeking out the first hint of movement. I had no idea of how well trained he would be. My only hope was that he was an amateur, coached for a set-up mission and that's all, with no skills and no instincts.

Unfortunately, life does not always go as we wish.

With my gaze so intent on the aisle and its rows of seats, I failed to notice the long expanse of luggage rack topping the compartment on each side. When I finally did catch the movement of the rack cover, it was too late.

The man flew out, timing his move to both release Wilhelmina from my hands and send me flying into one of the banks of seats. Wilhelmina was lost.

The only break I got was that the man was unarmed. Recovering my balance quickly, I used his own lack of footing to drive him into the seats behind me.

He hit the floor, and I landed on the armrests. This enabled me to rise first. I swung my legs into the aisle and backed off, ready to strike again.

The man was no amateur. With lightning-like speed, he was back on his feet, facing me down the aisle.

The initial shock stopped us both in our tracks.

It was like a mirror had been drawn across the aisle, both of us staring into the reflected side. He, too, was wearing one of M'Batti's guard uniforms. Obviously it was to be his ticket for tomorrow's events.

And then he grinned, that same kind of chilling grin that Robin must have faced back at the complex.

He was a pro, probably commando, and readiness to face me bordered on the sadistic. There was something almost spooky in his willingness to take me. For me, killing is a business, a necessity.

For this man, it was obviously a pleasure.

He moved slowly toward me, his body in perfect defensive position. I backed off slightly, edging my way toward a partition curtain behind me. If this jet was anything like the others that ferried us around Africa, I knew there would be an open bar area behind the curtain. If I was going to have to take this fanatic on, I preferred some operating room.

Apparently he shared my feelings, because no attempt was made to halt my backward progress. Once through the curtain, I backed to the far end of the area and planted myself, waiting for the first move to come.

I didn't have long to wait.

Almost as soon as he entered, he lunged for me. His style was strictly martial arts. His right leg swung, roundhouse style, for my head. A quick jab of my arm sent the limb flying over my head, but not without registering its impact on my forearm.

The man was good. Even before his lead foot had returned to earth, his following leg kicked toward me, catching me a glancing blow near the ribs. I darted left, avoiding the brunt of impact, and readied myself for his next move.

He charged instantly, his hands doing the work this time. I countered two quickly delivered blows, but failed to account for the man's determination. The blows were meant to fail. It was just his way of closing in on me. The completion of his attack was a well-placed slam of his forehead, directly onto the bridge of my nose.

For one brief second the world went black. I could feel the pain spreading across my cheeks and circling my head like a vice. My eyes watered over, turning the cabin into an aquatic nightmare.

I could feel the man's hands tighten on my wrists, and I knew he was coming in next with his knees. I waited. But for some reason the man was not pressing his advantage. Whether he was toying with me, or merely enjoying the sight of my agony, it was giving me the time I needed to think.

I had to do the unexpected.

My head was bursting from the impact of his blow, and he knew it. For that reason, I assumed it would be the last place he would look for retaliation. Without any regard for the further pain it would cause, I drove my face into him, hard, returning his suffering in kind.

It worked.

His hands slipped from me and his body reeled

backward as he tried to combat his own sudden blindness. I fired my leg out in the general direction of his body. I made contact but it was impossible for me to tell how much damage I had done.

I stumbled off to my right, my head desperately trying to shake off the affects of the collision. It would be a race now, as to who could see the other first.

The opportunity never realized itself. In the doorway behind us, I could hear Berenko enter the cabin.

The war was over. Seconds passed as both my double and I fought for clarity. He got there first.

"Kill him! For God's sake, Berenko, do it now!"

To my horror, the voice was as perfect a reproduction as the face. I struggled for something to say, that only Berenko and I could recognize, something to convince him that *I* was the real Nick Carter.

My second horror was in not getting the chance. The man lashed out once more with his feet, catching me full in the gut and knocking the wind clear out of me.

"What the hell are you waiting for?" shouted my double, as I sank to my knees.

To Berenko's credit, he held. Both of us stared at him. I could see him agonizing over which way to go. And then he spoke.

Horror number three.

"Perhaps I should just kill you both."

The air was still in response. Images of that night in Windhoek, when he almost failed to save me, flashed through my brain. I stared at him in helpless anticipation.

The moment was broken by the appearance of Robin. She took in the scene, registering her own uncertainty. I stared at her, silent messages screaming to her from my soul.

That's when the other guy goofed. He smiled. He tried to make it warm and gentle, but he failed. She had seen that smile, climbing down the barrel of a gun.

Without so much as a question in her face, she raised the barrel of her Sten, and ripped the man to shreds.

If there had been any air to spare in my lungs, I'm sure I would have sighed. Robin dropped her weapon and raced to me, doing her best to soothe the throbbing in my skull.

I stared at Berenko as he lowered his Sten and approached me.

"My apologies, Carter. You need never fear such behavior again. I owe you. My word as a professional . . . I owe you, and I shall repay my indiscretion in full."

I nodded my acceptance and struggled to my feet as Berenko turned and dispatched himself to the front of the plane to guide the crew toward our objective.

Kinshasa, and the end of the Society.

CHAPTER TWELVE

It was five o'clock in the morning, and faint ribbons of light were beginning to appear in the night sky. Berenko and I were huddled in a small park. Across the street from us was the stately mansion of the Zairan President. We had a clear view of the front gate.

Minutes before, Robin had passed through that gate, and now we were awaiting her return.

Berenko shifted nervously beside me. Neither one of us was feeling overconfident at the moment.

Brenko's doubts were the first to find voice. "I do not like this, my friend. We will be violating the sovereignty of an independent country."

"Do we have a choice?"

Berenko knew the answer. He heaved a giant sigh, and then perked to attention as Robin cleared the gate and made her way toward us. With one quick look behind her, she darted off the sidewalk and joined us in the sanctuary of our concealing shrubbery.

"They're in there," she gasped. "Two of them, at any rate . . . Nikumba, and your double." She gestured toward Berenko.

Berenko shook his head in apprehension.

"Is it the real Nikumba, or the double?" I asked.

Robin answered without the least hint of uncertainty. "The double. It has to be."

"How can you be sure?"

"Whenever Nikumba travels, he lets his double do all the public traveling. He disguises himself as a member of his own entourage, and lets his look-alike

191

deal with the mobs. He has always been aware of the possibility that there may be some real racist fanatic out there, ready to blow his brains out.''

"Smart man.''

"He usually travels along with his double, and when safe quarters are reached, he trades his disguise to the man and resumes his own identity. But last night, Nikumba and the other Berenko came here with only one female aide . . . the girl replacing me. The rest of the staff has been quartered elsewhere. My guess is that Nikumba continued on with the staff, leaving his double to handle the whole show . . . right up to his appearance on the podium.''

Berenko and I nodded our agreement.

"How will we locate the rest of the staff?'' I asked.

"Once we're inside, I'll lead you to the two men's rooms. While you're occupied with them, I'll talk to Jossina . . . that's the girl aide. She'll know the whole set-up, I'm sure.''

"That only leaves us the problem of how to get in,'' Berenko growled from beside me.

Robin flashed a big smile. "What problem? I'm Nikumba's chief aide . . . and a native Zairan to boot. The government people know me quite well, and you two are official Nikumba guards, uniforms and all. Getting in is simple. We just walk in!''

She turned and headed toward the gate. Berenko and I simply shrugged and followed her. The trip through the front entry was as simple and easy and she had predicted. We quickly made our way down a series of hallways, until a bank of three doors had been reached.

Robin pointed to each door and whispered her information to us. Berenko occupied door number one, Nikumba door two, and Robin's friend door three.

She gave me a quick, good-luck peck on the lips, and

disappeared behind the third door. Berenko and I then moved to door one.

Silently, we slid the door open and moved in. The faint light drifting in through the window lit the sleeping figure of Berenko's double. Both of us edged toward the bed, flanking on opposite sides. A silent agreement passed between us. If this double were anywhere near as well trained as the other had been, there was no room for mercy.

Once we were in position, I prodded the sleeping form with the butt of my Sten. He leaped up at the first hint of contact, his reflexes showing us our caution had been well founded.

But that's as far as he got. No sooner did he start to rise, than Berenko dispatched him with one calculated blow to the neck. The man slumped quietly back into his bed. He would not rise again.

I moved back to the door and kept an eye on the hall as Berenko stripped and re-dressed into the double's clothes. Then he rejoined me, and together we made our way to door number two.

Once more, we cracked open the unlocked entry and slipped soundlessly into the room. The Nikumba double, like his ally, was tucked safely in bed. We moved again, hoping to reply the scene just as it had gone previously.

This time, we would not be as lucky.

No sooner had we started to move, than a rumbling growl brought us both to a halt. From behind the bed strode the sleek, powerful form of the leopard.

The growling brought the slumbering figure to alertness. He leaped from the bed and threw on the lamp that stood next to him. Once more, Berenko and I found ourselves staring into the leopard's glistening fangs.

"What is it? What do you want?" came the

frightened voice of the bogus Nikumba.

I trained my gun on the cat, while Berenko leveled his on the man. Berenko did the talking.

"What is your name?"

The man seemed perplexed. "My name is Joseph Nikumba."

"And I'm Nicolai Lenin!" hissed the Russian. "We know you are not Nikumba. We have no desire to harm you. What is your *real* name?"

"I tell you, my name is Jos . . ." the man stammered.

"Don't be a fool! You are a security shield, a double. And in a few hours you are going to appear for the real Nikumba and deliver a speech. Unfortunately, your moment of glory is going to be cut short by an assassin's bullet!"

The man reacted to the knowledge of his own demise with an incredulous gasp. Berenko continued his verbal onslaught, not giving the man time to challenge him.

"Now, if you wish to see yourself murdered, that's your business. We are here to offer you an alternative. However, we can simply move the schedule up a bit, and eliminate you right now. You would prefer to die in bed?"

The man tried with great difficulty to swallow. "I would prefer not to die at all," he whispered.

"Call off the leopard, and we will talk, yes?"

He grabbed the hasp that held the animal's leash, his hand trembling visibly as the big cat strained toward the two intruders. For a fraction of a second, the man seemed to weigh the possibility of releasing the animal and taking his chances on escape.

"He won't get two feet before I cut him down," I warned. "And you'll be next."

"Do as they say, Kahif." It was Robin's voice from the doorway.

At the sight of her, the man seemed to relax a little. "Robin! Please, what's going on here?"

Her voice was like a soothing wind in the tenseness of the room. "These men are friends, Kahif. They mean you no harm. They are here to save your life, just as they have saved mine."

The man listened silently as Robin went on to explain the entire fabric of Nikumba's plan. I watched him carefully as Robin told him of his future. He believed her. With each revelation, his body would ease more and more into acceptance.

Finally he released the chain on the leopard, slumping back onto the bed as the certainty of her words brought reality to his confused brain.

A soft command sent the animal back behind the bed, and Berenko moved to the man, outlining the plans for the rest of the day, as I discussed the next step with Robin.

"What was your girlfriend able to tell you?"

"As I expected, the remainder of the crew is lodged at one of the downtown hotels. But I think we can ignore that."

"Why?"

"Jossina was asked to make two reservations; one for the hotel, and another for a residence, very near the speech site."

"What do you think it means?" I asked.

"The way I see it, the hotel is for the staff, but the house is M'Batti and his queen. He would want to be somewhere near the action, just to make sure it all goes as planned. But he would want himself removed from the main group. Once the supposed Nikumba is killed, the staff would be locked into the aftermath. M'Batti and Anene would no doubt like to be sure that they are in a position to depart as soon as events are concluded. They would not want to risk examination. M'Batti's disguise as one of his own staff would be too easily pierced.''

I stared in admiration at the girl's line of reasoning. ''You amaze me,'' I said softly.

She smiled in response. ''You should keep me around. I grow on you after a while!''

The thought was not unappealing.

Berenko broke the spell. ''He's ours. He'll cooperate, right down the line.''

''On the stand, and after?'' I asked.

''All the way. I'll stay here with him, and we'll work out exactly what is supposed to be said in public. The East-West formula will be tailored and delivered, just the way we want it.''

''Then we don't need the fake attempt on his life?''

''No,'' the big Russian answered. ''All we need now is for the real Nikumba to disappear off the face of the earth.''

I looked to Robin. ''And so he shall!''

She nodded her assent. ''And so he shall.''

''I don't wish to be negative,'' Berenko added. ''But M'Batti will no doubt be quite surrounded with protection. How do you propose to step by his inner guard?''

He was right. The house would be a far harder nut to crack. There was no walking in on that building. Robin was supposed to be dead, and my face would be very familiar, because of contact with my double, to the inner guard.

I looked to Robin. She was as uncertain as I. Her skills had reached their limit. It was now up to me. Berenko would have to remain with the double. Standing in the safety of the mansion, there were no answers. I would just have to find the house, and go from there.

I turned to Berenko. ''We'll just take one step at a time, Yuri. I'll get them. Trust me.''

He nodded. ''I just wish you had a small army to

assist you. It's going to be my life on that stand, too.''

"Yeah," I growled, "I wouldn't mind a division or two.''

"Wait!" Robin suddenly exclaimed. "We do have an army . . . or will have!"

We both stared at her as she drew a folded map from her pocket and thrust it into my hand.

"Here," she cried. "I've marked the house where Nikumba and Anene are staying. You should find it easily. Look it over. I'll join you there in . . .'' She checked the clock on the wall. ''. . in three hours!'' With that, she bolted for the door.

I looked at the clock's face. Three hours would be ten o'clock. That would only give us one hour till speech time. I tried to stop her.

"Where are you going?"

She turned briefly in the doorway. "Zaire is my home, remember? I was raised here. I've got friends.''

Before another question could be asked, she flew through the door and was gone.

I stood outside the house, pacing nervously. I had stationed myself down the street, using a recessed storefront to keep me from view. I looked into the store, staring, once more, at the clock that hung inside on the wall.

10:05.

Where the hell was Robin?

I had spotted the quarry one hour before. A light had come on in the forward part of the house, and a quick look-see had shown me M'Batti and Anene sitting in huddle conference.

No exterior guards had revealed themselves, and the room could be easily reached from the front entrance. All I needed now was for Robin to show with her friends.

10:09.

A glance up and down the street revealed nothing. In one direction, the streets were loaded with spectators, all making their way to the tiny park that held the podium. In the other direction, the podium itself could be seen. There were several workers making final adjustments on the microphones that would carry Berenko's and the bogus Nikumba's messages to the crowd.

But no Robin.

10:12.

There was no more time for waiting. I would just have to go it on my own. Steeling myself, I moved out into the stream of moving humanity, working myself across the street and breaking from the crowd at the entrance to the leader's lair, trusting my uniform to give me whatever advantage I might need.

I moved up the steps that led to the front door. I tried the knob. It was locked. Curling my fingers around the pistol in my right pocket, I squared my shoulders and rang the bell.

The door was answered by another uniformed soldier, rifle in hand.

I trusted my silencer and the noise of the crows behind me to drown out any attention-getting sounds. Before the man even had a chance to ask me "What for", I fired into his chest, sending him sprawling back into the hall.

Bursting through the door and stepping over his prostrate body, I leveled my gun down the hall. Two men stood at the end, surprise and alarm registering on their faces.

Before they could recover, I fired again. The two men crumpled beneath the salvo, joining their buddy in eternal slumber.

Slamming the door behind me, I turned toward the first room on my right. Without even testing the lock, I fired into it. The door flew open under the heel of my boot and I used the momentum to carry me on into the room.

Anene stood in the middle of the room, her bottom half covered in native splendor, her top half as naked as the day I had first seen her. She blinked her astonishment at me as she tried to figure out my presence.

"Where's Nikumba?" I hissed, allowing her to study the barrel of my Sten.

It was that moment that recognition dawned. She had assumed me to be my double, and now she understood. It was me she was facing.

"Carter!"

"Very astute, Your Highness. Now, where is Nikumba?"

"I know no Nikumba."

"Don't be cute. Your boyfriend . . . M'Batti, or whatever he's calling himself today . . . where is he?"

The Black Goddess drew herself up to her full height, her breasts reaching out in front of her like twin invitations. She smiled warmly, seductively, as she spoke. "We underestimated you, Carter. You are truly a resourceful man." She moved forward a step, and my gun rose to halt her progress.

"Time is growing short, Your Highness, and I'm in no mood for amenities. Where is M'Batti?"

She paused, still smiling, and her hand moved to the clasp that held her native skirt, and then released it. The colored fabric dropped to the floor, leaving her quite naked.

"As you can see, I am unarmed, Mr. Carter. Perhaps we could talk a moment?"

I was staring at a black Venus, sculptured in onyx, a rippling, muscular statue created by a master. It was a clever diversion, and I knew it, but it was still hard to take my eyes off the sheer perfection of her naked form.

"There is room for you, Carter," she breathed. "There is room in the new empire for daring men." Her hands began moving over the firm, flat plane of her belly. "Join us, Carter. Work with us. Share your strength. Share it with the cause. Share it with me." The hands moved slowly, accenting the chocolate silkiness of her flesh, working their way down to the defiant tuft of hair that topped her sex. "Look. See what can be yours if you join us in our effort!"

Her voice was hypnotic, not to mention the pure delight of her body. She was advancing slowly, carefully, closer and closer to me.

"Power, Carter," she purred. "Power can be yours. I can be yours!"

And that's where the love affair ended. With a sudden jerk of her hand, she tried to wrench the gun from my grasp. I slammed the butt of the Sten into her wrist, and she reeled away, her voice suddenly exploding into a barrage of clicks and stops . . . that same musical language that I had heard Bosima use in Algiers.

As she reached the center of the room, a door in the far wall burst open. In it stood two of the Watusi elite.

I fired, leveling the two men who were trying to make their way through. Behind me, I could hear the commotion of more soldiers rattling their way down the hall. It was time to depart.

I backed my way toward the window. Anene was quick to figure out my plans. She shouted more orders, no doubt directing the men at the door to head me off. It was the last order she ever gave.

My Sten blast hit her square in the chest and sent her flying back over one of the room's tables. Quickly I turned and threw open the window, diving through it to the ground below.

Scrambling to my feet, I ran, weaving my way toward the back of the house, hoping like hell I could stay ahead of the pursuit.

Just about the time I felt as though I had it made, the party seemed to come to an end. In front of me, the walkway suddenly filled with two eight-foot forms.

I froze.

A quick look behind me confirmed more bad news. Two more Watusi's had sealed off the other end, while another two found their way through the window I had just exited.

I raised my gun toward the two nearest giants. If I was going down, I'd be damned if it was going to be alone. I zeroed in on their faces, ready to send them into whatever after-world a Watusi readies for.

What I saw, however, froze me in my tracks. I was staring at two eight-foot giants, yes, but the faces that greeted me in return were the faces of . . . ten-year-old children.

And the face on my left winked.

CHAPTER THIRTEEN

What occurred next was enough to make me challenge my sanity. The two baby-faced guards moved toward me, fanning out and approaching me on each side. The whole time they watched the guards behind me, ignoring me entirely.

I turned and saw the four other Watusi's moving in with menace in their hearts. Once they had me flanked, the two baby-faces halted. There was a sudden movement, and from what should have been their bellies, emerged two slender reeds of wood. There was the barest sound of air, and two of the approaching Watusi's found themselves crumbling to the earth.

The other two guards halted in amazement. And then they caught their bearings. Their rifles went up, ready to blow me and my two sudden allies in half. But before they could fire, the Watusi's on each side of me seemed to fall in half for them. The two robes suddenly flew from their bodies, and what had been two eight-foot giants, suddenly revealed itself to be four, four-foot children.

Robin's army had arrived. Pygmies!

Of course! Those tiny denizens of the Zairan rain forests had no doubt been Robin's playmates as a child. And here they stood, impersonating their enemy, one tiny four-foot frame being carried by another!

The four pygmies moved like acrobats. Before the two remaining Watusi's could overcome their surprise, the four little men rolled. The miniature bodies hit the ground, and twisted up to their knees, blowguns pumping for all they were worth.

The last two Watusi's jerked as the deadly poison of

the darts poured instantly into their systems.

And then, silence. The four elfin natives leaped to their feet, their voices chattering bird-like in victory. From behind me came other voices, sharing in their delight. I turned and saw Robin, beaming in victory.

"What do you think of my army?" she grinned, coming to me.

There was nothing I could say. I just kissed her, bringing on a burst of giggling from the imps behind me. Robin smiled, and then broke from me, shouting commands to her regiment. They answered in kind, and ran off down the courtway.

"Care to translate?" I asked, shaking my head in amazement.

"I told them to round up the others and start securing the podium. Their blowguns will eliminate the Watusi guard with little attention being drawn, and then they will climb into the robes and replace the eight-foot bulk with their four-foot bodies."

I couldn't suppress a chuckle. "Did I ever tell you you were brilliant?"

"Yes," she grinned. "But it could bear repeating."

"More brilliant than I, I'm afraid," I said, growing sober once again. "I missed M'Batti. Anene has been taken care of, but the main man is still on the loose."

"I know. We arrived just as the action started. I saw M'Batti fade around the corner at the end of the street. I sent two of the pygmies after him, and stayed here to make sure you got through okay."

"Thanks. Let's see how your friends did."

I moved off after her. We circled behind the house, and down toward the end of the block. No sooner had we rounded the corner, than the fate of Robin's friends confronted us.

Two tiny forms lay helpless on the ground. I heard the breath catch in Robin's throat as she spied her first casualties. The sight of them even sent a chill down my spine. They had been hit by the exploding shells.

"Jesus," I hissed, "he's got the rifle. The son of a bitch is going to try to nail the double himself!"

Robin twisted her face from the sight, burying herself into my shoulder. I wanted to comfort her, but there was just no time to waste. I had to get to the podium and let Berenko know that M'Batti was on the loose.

"Listen, love," I said. "We're going to have casualties. Don't think about it. Just *move!* Search the crowd. You know M'atti's disguise. Try to flush him out. I'm going to warn Berenko. If you find him, nail him, right on the spot!"

"Don't worry," she answered, her eyes traveling once more to the two fallen children. "I'll know what to do with him."

I had no doubt she would.

We moved off down the street. As we joined the crowd in the park, Robin peeled off to do her job, giving my hand a quick squeeze before disappearing into the throng.

I worked my way up to the podium, and caught Berenko's attention. He drifted over to me.

"How do we stand?"

"On one leg at the moment. I got Anene, but M'Batti slipped through the net."

Berenko heaved a sigh and brushed a few beads of sweat from his brow. "Did Robin's army ever materialize?"

I smiled and pointed out one of the nearby Watusi's. Berenko studied the face, and grunted at the surprising innocence of the features.

"Pygmies!" I chirped. "They'll have the podium covered in a matter of minutes. Robin is searching the crowd for M'Batti, but I don't think she'll find him."

Berenko returned his attention to me. "Why not?"

"He's got the rifle, Yuri. He intends to pull the whole thing off on his own. I don't think he'll be anywhere near the crowd. I'm going to watch those windows, but I doubt if I'll be able to head him off. Any ideas?"

Berenko followed my gaze to the row of buildings overlooking the park and the dais. There was nothing to be seen in any window.

It was Berenko's decision, and I knew it. He could get off the podium now, or take his chances with the speeches. The speeches were vital. The words had to be said. But we would then be gambling on the assassination we so desperately needed to avoid.

I let Berenko roll it around. My eyes circled the crowd, finally coming to rest on the cage at the far right end of the podium. In it were two of the leopards that seemed to always accompany Nikumba. They were pacing the narrow confines, their amber eyes staring hungrily into the mass of people surrounding them. I felt a sudden kinship with them.

We were all four . . . the cats, and Berenko and I . . . survivors, looking for the kill.

Berenko's voice came in to break my thoughts.

"Just give me time. We must speak. Watch those windows. At the first sign of trouble, fire. Just give me a second to get Nikumba's double under cover."

I admired the man. I nodded my assent and quickly lifted the silencer from the end of my gun. That would be Berenko's signal. I slipped a fresh clip into the Sten, and shook the Russian's hand. "Looks like we get our attempt after all."

He nodded. "Let's just hope it's unsuccessful."

He moved back toward the lectern, and I moved off to my left. I stationed myself a little way off, at the base of a nearby tree, and scanned the banks of windows overlooking the park.

Berenko was called to the podium, and began addressing the crowd. I studied him briefly. His eyes were flickering from audience to background, searching for the first sign of trouble. From behind the lectern, I could see him easing the Walther from inside his coat, readying it in the firm grip of his hand.

I returned my gaze to the windows, and settled in for the events. Berenko's speech was without incident. He returned to his chair and plopped himself beside the bogus Nikumba. Another speaker took the stand and began the introductions for the main event. Nikumba was seconds from the microphone.

And then it caught my eye.

One of the windows had moved. Only slightly, but I was sure that it had not been open before. My hands tensed over the grip of the Sten and I began moving forward, following a route from tree to tree.

I moved to a spot where one branch of a tree joined the trunk. I set up the Sten, using the branch to fix my aim on the glass.

Almost imperceptibly, the window crept up one . . . two . . . three more inches.

Nikumba's name rang out over the loudspeaker, and the crowd suddenly burst into life. A fear crept over me that perhaps Berenko would not hear the gunfire.

But it was too late to worry about that. A rifle barrel now appeared on the window sill, pointed directly at the lectern, and the double only inches away.

I fired the Sten, my finger glued to the trigger. The second floor window burst into pieces. Glass exploded inward and, to my relief, the gun barrel jerked erratically as I emptied the entire clip.

Near me, people were looking over and then backing away as the certainty of my actions hit home. But the crowd beyond them was still roaring . . . the deafening roar of an adoring mob.

As quickly as I could, I shed the spent clip from my gun, inserting a new one as I checked the podium for response. Berenko still sat, and the Nikumba double was waving innocently at his admirers.

They hadn't heard the shooting.

Panic seized me as I realized the gun in the window was trying to pick up where it had left off. The crowd was just too loud. Berenko would never get the warning. I fired another quick burst, and the rifle once more dipped erratically.

But time was on M'Batti's side. I was into my final clip. Once it was gone, the double would be a sitting duck. I needed to create a sudden and complete panic. I had to get Berenko's attention . . . and fast!

I searched the grounds desperately for some idea. And then my eyes lit on the cage with the two leopards. A single lock secured the door. I had a clear shot. There was only a second of hesitation as the consequences of my choice ran through my brain.

With those two cats loose, there would be total chaos. Innocent lives might be lost. But what choice did I have?

It was between a few civilians, or an Africa gone mad, with the killing of thousands of whites as its price.

There was no choice.

Another quick glance at the window showed me the rifle finding its way to the target. I raised the Sten and blew the lock off the cage. The lock burst into fragments, and the force of the blast sent the cage door flying open.

Suddenly the crowd grew still. The cats had recoiled from the shattering of their cage. But the sight of the open door, and freedom, was beginning to overcome their initial fear.

The screams started at the point nearest the cage, and then began spreading through the crowd as the realization of the danger spread.

Men and women began moving, terror driving them into panicked retreat. I shot my eyes to the podium. At the first signs of panic in the crowd, Berenko seemed to get the message. He dove for the fake Nikumba, taking the man in a tackle.

The round black man hit the platform rudely. A second later, the lecturn he had been stand at burst into shreds of wood as two exploding shells smashed into its face. I turned and emptied the remainder of my clip into the window.

To my great relief, the rifle fell this time, dropping two stories down to the ground. I dropped the Sten, withdrew Wilhelmina from my uniform, and raced toward the building that housed the assassin. It was difficult to weave my way through the mass of panicked bodies. By now the leopards had found their way out of their prison, and the crowd was retreating in total terror.

It took a few seconds, but finally I reached the doorway. Robin appeared at exactly the same moment I did.

"Stay here," I shouted. "I think I may have hit him. Just watch this door. I don't want you in danger."

"The hell I will!" The determination in her voice made me pause for an instant. "I want him, Nick! As bad as you. It's my country . . . my Africa he tried to pervert. I've earned a shot at him!"

There was no time to argue, and her resolve showed me I would have gotten nowhere even if I had tried.

"All right," I said. "But stay behind me, and keep that gun ready!"

She nodded and followed me into the building. The screaming grew distant as we entered a wide lobby. Off to the left was a flight of steps. I moved quickly and cautiously, my eyes glued to the landing above.

The first landing was made without mishap. We then took the same cautious climb to the second floor. Still no M'Batti. I was hoping like hell that my last blast at the window had done the work. We hit the second landing, and I peered around the corner.

Down the hall, at about the exact spot where the room should be, a door stood half open. The remainder of the hall was pitch black, the only light coming from behind the open door. The hall was deadly still and quiet. Only the faint murmuring of the crowd outside interrupted the stillness.

I edged out into the hall, and Robin followed. We slowly moved toward the door. I was certain that the pounding of my heart could be heard, giving me away. As we neared the door, all progress halted.

I felt it, suddenly . . . an instinct . . . another heartbeat . . . not really audible, but sensed and felt. It was behind me, and it wasn't Robin.

Realization came far too late.

The darkness behind me suddenly filled with the harsh echo of a gunblast. The shell caught me on the side of the shoulder. It was just a grazing wound, but with enough impact to send Wilhelmina flying down the hall. Robin started to turn, but the commanding voice of M'Batti stopped her.

"Don't make me shoot you, child. Drop the gun. Slip it slowly and carefully over the railing, and drop it."

She had no choice but to obey. The gun clattered as it tumbled down the steps.

"You can both turn now. Your destinies await you."

Muttering angrily under my breath, I turned until I faced M'Batti, now lit by the light spilling up the stairwell. He paused at the head of the stairs, ready to make his departure, but not before he had taunted us with his victory.

"So, Mr. Carter, it seems you almost saved the day."

"There is no body, M'Batti. You're little scheme is useless. Why don't you just throw it in?"

He laughed. "I think not. We have other plans, all of them brilliant, all of them mine."

"You're finished, M'Batti!" I shouted. "We've got your double. We own him, and there's not a damn thing you can do about it!"

His confident manner shattered a bit, but the smile quickly returned. "Yes, it would seem that Nikumba will be lost to us. But M'Batti will be born, anyway. My surgeons will create the new figure of African unity. There *will* be a new Africa, Mr. Carter. You will not be able to stop it."

I wanted to continue taunting him, buying time, but the pain in my right shoulder was beginning to take its toll. M'Batti merely stared, that idiotic smile glued to his face. He was enjoying the little bit of victory he had been able to snatch from the day's events.

But time was running out. His pistol was beginning to find its way toward me, the barrel planting itself on a line with my chest. I had no more words.

But Robin did.

"Please, Joseph. Don't kill him. He won't do anything, I promise you."

M'Batti laughed. "Is that so, Mr. Carter? You would just walk away and leave me to my primitive devices?"

We both knew the answer to that one.

"You see, my child," he said to Robin. "Mr. Carter has his duties. To America, to Imperialism, to Mr. Berenko. He will no more turn his back on African enslavement than I on its liberation." His eyes grew hard and cold as they narrowed on her face. "It is you, child, that I cannot forgive. Why have you deserted me?"

In spite of events, I could see Robin's anguish at the accusation.

The little girl was trying to reach her Father.

"I have deserted nothing, Joseph. Africa for Africans has been my goal, and it always will be."

"Then why have you aided our enemies?"

"It is you who have become the enemy. The cause is still just. I will continue to work for a free Africa, under African governments. But I cannot let myself become like the enemy we fight. A free Africa should become a model for the world, a model of peace and freedom. Models show the world, Joseph, they do not conquer it."

M'Batti's composure seemed to slip. "You are a child! What do you know of the world? *I* shall tell you what is good and what is not. You dare to tell *me* what is good for Africa?"

"Yes!" she screamed. "I fight for the people of Africa. You fight only for your own maniacal power! I do not believe that an Africa that enslaves others is worth existing!"

M'Batti's voice was chilling as he spoke. "You will not be alive to debate it, I'm afraid."

In his anger, the pistol swung toward Robin. If that was her intention, I could not have been more grateful. I tensed myself, ready to fly at the crazed ruler before he could shoot.

But none of us was to have our way. At that moment, from the landing below, came the horrifying rumble of a leopard's growl. The animal must have followed his master's scent.

M'Batti's eyes leaped down the stairs. His voice cut through the silence of the hall, shouting his commands to the beast below. He was answered with a loud roar that sounded anything but obedient. For one second, Nikumba's eyes widened. I saw terror in them.

He shouted again, and for the moment the stairs

seemed to silence. The look of fear was replaced by one of understanding, and then glee.

"He senses blood, Mr. Carter. I believe it is your blood he smells. That is truly unfortunate. I shall have to kill him. No cat can remain in captivity who has tasted human blood."

"You're breaking my heart," I hissed.

A sadistic smile broke out on his lips. Carefully, with one eye still down the steps, he moved from the head of the stairway.

"Vadu has always been my favorite pet," he spat. "But since he must die, it is only fair he get a last meal. Please, Mr. Carter, I wish you to walk down those steps."

In answer, another rumbling roar carried up from the stairwell. My belly iced over at the thought of facing death at the leopard's jaws.

"You're not moving, Mr. Carter."

"I think I'll stay right here, if you don't mind. The gun would be quicker."

Suddenly the gun rose up and leveled itself at Robin's face.

"Either you move, Mr. Carter, or you get the privilege of seeing your lady's brains spilled over the hall."

I thought a moment. "All right," I replied. "You win."

"Nick, *no!*" Robin screamed.

There were tears in her eyes, tears for me, tears for Nikumba, tears for all she had believed in. My heart sank as I stared into all the misery that engulfed her. It was not the way I wished to go, but if there was half a chance that he would spare Robin, I had to take it.

Her eyes bored into me, sensing the directions of my thought. And then the agony fled from her eyes. In its place came a silent wave of love, and the hard edge of resolve. Before I could even say, "No!", she darted toward M'Batti.

I watched in horror as the gun in M'Batti's hand barked to life. He fired twice, and twice the fabric of Robin's blouse burst at her back. But she did not fall.

She slammed into him, driving him into the wall. And then she attacked. Her nails came up like ten sharp knives and dug into his face. A scream erupted from his throat as her fingers tore into the flesh of his cheeks. He dropped the gun, his hands coming up to flail at the source of his torment.

He twisted himself, trying to escape her fury, but Robin would not yield. The two of them struggled, with Robin carefully pushing him toward the edge of the stairwell.

I too moved. I raced toward the fallen pistol, praying that I could make it before events got too far.

But Robin's determination far exceeded mine. On the very edge of the stairs, she gave a final lunge. M'Batti's foot slipped from the landing, and the hard force of her body drove both of them over the brink. The two crashed to the stairs.

A bellowing roar from the bottom answered the sound of their collapse. I managed to get the gun into my hand, but ignored it as I dove to try and capture Robin's retreating ankle.

I nailed it, halting her fall at the head of the steps. M'Batti was not so lucky. His fall carried him, blood streaming down his cheeks, into the waiting jaws of the leopard.

Another roar, and one long, loud piercing scream, told the remainder of the story. I struggled with Robin, pulling her back onto the landing. There was little strength left in her to help me. It took a second, but finally she was stretched out on the relative safety of the floor.

I left her for a moment, and moved to the landing, taking aim on the cat. The initial sight turned my stomach. Below, the beast was feasting on his master. Death is an ever-present part of the spy business, but sometimes, no matter how much you try to insulate yourself, death has its impact.

I was staring at the lifeless form of Joseph Nikumba/M'Batti. His face had been reduced to hamburger.

The bile was rising in my throat as I fired into the bulk of fur below. Two shots were all it took. The leopard's skull deteriorated into nothingness.

I lowered the pistol and took a calming breath. It was Robin's shallow moan that finally brought me back to normalcy.

I moved to her, a silent prayer of hope on my lips. I quickly tried to assess the damage. Her body had been pierced twice. By the look of it, my prayers would remain unanswered.

Robin knew it was over.

"Nick," she whispered, her voice faint and far-away, "I did it. I got him, didn't I?"

"You got him, love," I murmured, stroking the matted hair from her lovely face.

"He called me weak, Nick. He said my weakness was his ally. You remember."

I shook my head in agreement, wanting to quiet her. But there was no point. The end was coming, and she knew it.

"I'm not weak, Nick. I had to show him. I had to . . ."

Her talk disappeared in a cry of pain. It took a second for it to pass.

"Is that why you helped us?" I asked.

"You know better." Her eyes bore into me. "People, Nick. People are what matter. Philosophies

can be hated. Communism, capitalism, colonialism
. . . these can all deserve hatred. Not people. People
must be judged for what they are. I judged you, Nick
. . . not your country.''

"And?"

A useless question. This time her answer was not in
words. She smiled through her pain and leaned into me,
her lips planting themselves softly on mine. The kiss
lingered, broken only by another spasm of pain shooting through her.

The light was fading in those olive eyes.

"Nick?"

"What, love?"

"Would you have gone with me? Would you have
tried, forever?"

I stared at her, but I did not have to consider my
answer. "Yes!"

She smiled, a deep, satisfied smile, and then the light
expired.

I heard footsteps on the stairs below, but I ignored
them. Berenko climbed the steps slowly, his mind
grasping the events instantly. A hard knot of pain rested
in my belly, threatening to find its way into my emotions.

The only thing that saved me from the embarrassment of emotion was the echoing reminder of Berenko's words . . . *"Feelings, Mr. Carter. Feelings are
a luxury!"*

I gripped myself, swallowing the feelings before
they could ever find life. Berenko's hand came down to
clasp my shoulder in sympathy and understanding. I
took strength from the gesture, and finally found the
courage to face him.

I looked him square in the eye.

A tear was crawling down his cheek.

Berenko and I were sharing a drink on the deserted veranda of a chalet, near Zurich. The chill wind was circling around us, swept down from the snow-covered peaks of the surrounding Alps. It was a farewell drink we were sharing, but the mood was anything but comradely.

Robin still hung heavily in my thoughts.

With great sensitivity, Berenko tried to cut through my moroseness.

"She died bravely, my friend. Allow her memory to be a bright one."

I looked at him and nodded, managing a weak smile. "What's to become of our new Nikumba?" I asked.

"As you already know, he is being controlled by an East-West committee, made up of representatives of both our governments. The last report I heard was that the East-West formula would be refined, and then fed to him. He will then promote it, and quietly retire from public life. He will use the assassination attempts as his motive for retreat."

"You know," I mused, "it really is a shame that the real Nikumba had to go off the deep end. His ideas were valid . . . brilliant, in fact. I really believe the man could have pulled Africa together."

"Of that, there is no doubt. The ironic thing is that, although M'Batti is dead, his ideas will go on. The committee is studying them even now, to see which ones can be used to serve Africa's emergence."

I sipped at my drink. "What will become of the interim council he was to lead?"

"The white government will continue in South Africa, until a new black candidate can be found. Nikumba will be sorely missed.''

In spite of myself, I laughed. ''Odd, isn't it? We've made a hero out of a madman.''

Berenko, too, laughed. ''I'm afraid, my friend, it will not be the first time.''

Another silence descended as both of us finished our drinks. Then Berenko rose to his feet.

''You're leaving?'' I asked.

''I must.'' His hand reached out to me and I accepted it warmly. ''An unlikely marriage, you and I. Is that not so, Mr. Carter?''

''I would never have thought we'd be working together. But it was an honor, Yuri. One that made me very nervous, at times, but an honor.''

His face reddened slightly at the remainder of his indiscretions. ''Please,'' he said. ''I intend to keep my promise to you. I owe you, my friend, and I shall make good on that debt in some way.''

I shook his hand again. ''So,'' I said, ''it would seem we are once more enemies.''

Berenko smiled. ''I prefer the term adversaries. It gives us both the respect we deserve. For enemies, one has hatred. For you, I only have regard.''

I nodded my agreement, and Berenko moved off. But he only got two or three steps before halting. He turned to me, his face showing slight discomfort.

''I have one more question, Mr. Carter. I do not wish to pry. Your talents with women have more than proved themselves to me on this mission. But I could not help overhearing your final conversation with the girl. Would you have gone with her?''

I shook my head no.

''You could lie to someone, on their deathbed?''

I thought a moment before answering. ''I've always

understood why the dying tell the truth. It lets them enter the afterworld with a lighter soul. But I've never understood why they *ask* the truth. I saw no reason to make her burdens any heavier.''

Berenko grunted, and then smiled. ''Adversaries,'' he said. ''We could never be anything more. Good luck, my friend . . . and goodbye.'' And he walked away.

I watched him disappear around the veranda, and silently wished him well. My eyes then traveled back to the surrounding peaks. Robin's face, smiling and warm, just as it had been on that trip across North Africa, flashed through my mind.

''Let her memory be a bright one.''

I slipped a few bills from my pocket and rose from the table.

Today would be a good day to try out that new pair of skis.